SHIFT OF FATE

A WOLFGUARD PROTECTORS NOVEL

KIMBER WHITE

NOKAY PRESS LLC

For all the latest on my new releases and exclusive content, sign up for my newsletter. http://bit.ly/241Wcf

CHAPTER ONE

Val

The mountains drew me. Stark. Beautiful. Their snow-capped peaks disappearing into a mist-shrouded sky. They reminded me of home.

Home. It was odd that I still called it that. I left Russia nearly twenty years ago when I was just a teenager. But, I had been driven away. Forced into exile by a ruthless wolf pack leader who ordered every member of my family dead, one by one. My older brother Andre got me out in the middle of the night, but only just barely. I still bore the scars from where the dragonsteel bullet had pierced my shoulder.

But all that was behind us now. It took a generation, but Andre had found a way to claw back what had been taken from us. He returned to Russia and now led the most powerful pack across the Atlantic...arguably in the world.

I could have joined him. He offered. I could take my place alongside him. It was tempting. Every once in a while, I dreamed about going home.

But, there was something different for me. I felt it in my bones. It stirred inside me, calling to my wolf, only I hadn't yet been able to find it.

Now, sitting in the company SUV with the darkly tinted windows concealing my eyes, I stared out at the Rocky Mountains and dreamed of my first homeland. And I wondered if I'd made the wrong decision after all.

"Val?" the voice cut through to me, snapping my thoughts to the present.

"You still there?"

I leaned over and turned up the speaker volume. "I'm here, Leo. Sorry about that."

Leo was my nephew. One of four. I had a niece as well, Grace, but she wasn't a shifter like we were. They had all stayed behind like I did when Andre went back to assume the mantle of Kalenkov pack leader. They stayed for themselves and for me. We found good work here. A purpose. Today though, I was having trouble remembering what that was.

"I asked you if you've seen her yet?" Leo asked.

I peered below the visor. I parked in a shaded spot across from a high-rise apartment building in downtown Denver. It was oddly quiet here at the moment. Clean. Rich. I had my eyes on the front lobby. A uniformed bellman stood sentry wearing crisp, white gloves. He dipped his chin and smiled as every pedestrian walked by. He was good. Jovial. But, I could sense him cataloging every face as they passed, just like I was.

"No," I said. "She hasn't come out yet."

"How long are you going to wait?"

I tapped my phone screen. It was just past one in the afternoon. I should have been on the road an hour ago.

"I'm about done waiting," I answered, trying to keep the anger out of my voice. But, Leo knew me too well.

"I'm sorry," he said. "I should have told Payne I'd take this one for you. I can't figure why he didn't send one of the newbies."

"Because he said it was important," I answered. It was the thing I'd been telling myself over and over, trying to keep the edge of rage out of my mind.

"Important," Leo said. "It's a glorified babysitting job, Val. It's beneath you. It's beneath all of us at this point."

I held my tongue. Leo was saying all the things I thought. But, it wasn't going to do me a damn bit of good whining.

"Boss asked for me specifically," I said. "It means he had a reason."

"What's her name again?" Leo asked.

I kept my eyes glued to the lobby doors. I had already memorized the case file.

"Willow Rousseau," I said to Leo.

"Rousseau," Leo parroted. "Right. Did you check into her family? Because I did. Her dad's a made guy. One of the New Jersey families."

I knew all of that too. It was the first question I asked of Payne Fallon, my boss. For the past year, I'd moved up the ranks at Wolfguard Inc. We were an elite, private security firm. Payne's clientele ranged from Fortune 500 companies, to A-list actors, to heads of state.

And he'd promised me a piece of it. A full partnership. I hadn't yet told that to Leo or any of my other nephews. I wasn't sure how they'd feel about me becoming one of their bosses. Considering my current circumstances, I was pretty sure Leo might think Payne was stringing me along.

A glorified babysitting gig. Leo wasn't wrong.

"Rousseau's not the client," I said, almost as if I were trying to convince myself, not him. "The girl's fiancé is. The Soren family. I don't know what the bigger picture is, but it's not my job to know it for right now. Payne wants me to get her to his place near the Chesapeake Bay in one piece."

Leo sighed. "Long drive, man. Why can't we just put her on a plane?"

"Because that's the way Soren wants it," I said.

"When will you be back in Chicago?" Leo asked.

"Three days, tops," I said. "I have a meeting with Payne on the seventh."

"Something you want to share with the rest of the class?"

I smiled. Leo was fishing. Of course I was a fool to think he hadn't already figured out I was up to something. If this job went off without a hitch, I expected Payne to follow through on offering me a partnership. I hadn't yet decided whether I would run it by the rest of my family before I accepted. For now, there was no point pondering. It wasn't a done deal until it was a done deal. And I had this three-day babysitting gig to finish first.

"Well, if you need anything, just shoot me a text," Leo said. "I'm in Vegas this week for the Lyndon job. Erik and Edward are down in Cabo and Milo is...hell...I don't know where Milo is."

"He's tracking a rogue bear somewhere in Washington State," I said "Bastard's killed three or four people. Local cops are out of their depth."

"Yeah," Leo said. There was something wistful in his tone. Bounty hunting was his calling as much as Milo's. I knew it irked him not to go along on this job. Come to think of it, Leo had been restless a lot lately, just like he was now.

"I'll call you when I finish things up in Virginia," I said. "You're due for some R and R. I suggest you take it."

Leo made a noise low in his throat. He knew better than to

argue with me though. Instead, he said a terse goodbye and wished me good luck.

Luck. Skill. This job had nothing to do with any of that. My wolf was restless, and that's the thing I wouldn't say to Leo or any of the others. Business suits, earpieces, SUVs. They all had their place, but I itched to get out in the woods and just go feral for a while. My wolf had needs. I wanted to go somewhere I couldn't hear the city sounds and where the stars dazzled by the millions, freed from all the light pollution.

The mountains. God. That's where I wanted to go. But first, there was the job.

I checked the time again. We were now an hour and a half behind schedule. I had half a mind to storm into the building and throw this woman over my shoulder. I knew the type. Young socialite. Lived on her daddy's dime from day one. She was probably standing in front of a closet full of shoes right now, intent on picking out something wholly inappropriate, impractical, and likely to break her ankles.

I picked the case file up from the passenger seat.

Willow Rousseau. I had her head shot clipped to the front of it. Pretty. Green eyes and brown hair with an auburn tinge to it. The photo was a studio glamor shot. In it, she wore too much damn makeup that made her look probably twenty years older than she really was. She had those silly pouty lips in it. I knew if I pulled up her social media profiles, I'd find an array of pretentious selfies. Willow on a yacht. Willow in some club wearing expensive clothes she didn't earn money to pay for.

Oh, she had future trophy wife written all over her. Her fiancé Jason Soren came from huge, old money. I did my research. Soren's father made it from oil and gas over a century ago. The Astors and Rockefeller club for sure.

But Willow, her family's money was new and probably precarious. Her father Daniel Rousseau owned a construction company in New Jersey. Little Willow was most definitely marrying up.

The trouble was, Rousseau had made plenty of enemies along the way. So had Soren. I could almost feel sorry for Willow getting caught up in the middle of it. Almost.

Payne said the family had received a couple of death threats. Just last month, Wolfguard had unraveled a kidnapping plot. Apparently, Willow didn't even know she was the target. My job, among other things, was to keep it that way. Rousseau and Soren didn't want their precious jewel to worry her little head about the big bad world out there.

So, my job was simple. Get the girl from her apartment in Denver to Soren's house near the Chesapeake Bay. Easy. Boring. But, important. Payne didn't have to tell me that Soren was one of his most lucrative clients. It's probably why I was sitting here instead of one of the newbies. Payne couldn't afford any mistakes on this one.

Two thirty rolled around and I officially lost my patience.

"Son of a bitch," I muttered. I tucked the case file under the seat, slid on my aviator sunglasses and slammed the car door behind me. I buttoned my suit jacket and crossed the street.

I got a friendly nod from the bellman. "Good afternoon, sir," he said. "Visiting someone in the building? I can have the desk manager ring up for you."

I pulled out a business card and handed it to him. The bellman's eyes widened just a touch, but his smile didn't falter.

"I'm here for Ms. Rousseau," I said.

"You're her driver?" he asked, his expression puzzled.

I let out a sigh that almost turned into a growl. "Something like that," I said.

He handed the card back. "Does she know to expect you?"

"She knows," I said.

He must have read something on my face. "I see," he said. "I'm afraid Ms. Rousseau has a bit of a habit keeping people like you waiting."

I resisted the urge to tell him Ms. Rousseau had likely never met anyone like me in her whole life.

"Anyway," I said. "I need to go knock on her door, it appears."

His brow went up. I watched the man work something out for himself. He gave me a knowing glance. In me, he probably thought he just saw another hired hand. A lackey. A kindred spirit in that, maybe. I had a distinct feeling Willow Rousseau had tried his patience a time or two as well.

"Look, mate," he said. "I could let you up. But, it won't do any good."

"I'll be the judge of that," I said, starting to brush past him. He put a hand on my arm. My muscles went rigid.

That poor bellman. He couldn't know what I was. But, on some instinctive level, I know he sensed it. He dropped his hand from me.

"What I mean is," he said. "Ms. Rousseau is already gone. She went that way about thirty seconds before you walked up here."

He pointed down the sidewalk. This time, I couldn't hold back the growl.

"How the hell..." I didn't bother to finish the sentence. Dammit. My eyes never left that door. I'd only seen four people come out. None of them looked a thing like Willow Rousseau.

I palmed a twenty and shook the bellman's hand. Then, I took off down the street moving as fast as I dared.

She might have gotten past me, but instinct was on my side. The moment I saw her, I knew.

She had on a pink knit beanie pulled low. No five-inch

ridiculous heels. Instead, she had on ripped jeans, an over-sized t-shirt and worn Chuck Taylors.

"Willow!" I shouted, my voice low. It was getting even harder to keep my growl and my wolf at bay.

She turned. She looked nothing like her picture at all. She had a fire behind her eyes that flipped my heart and stirred my wolf.

She snarled. She knew exactly who I was and what I was doing here.

"Well," she said. She rolled her eyes and took a step toward me. "You planning on just standing there, or are you gonna throw me over your shoulder and give me a spanking?"

My mouth dropped. The air went out of me. Then, I really did growl.

CHAPTER TWO

WILLOW

ONE HOUR EARLIER...

He wasn't going to stop calling. I could let it go to voicemail maybe once, but then there would be a knock on my door.

I stood in the doorway to my bedroom. Or no...my former bedroom. There was nothing left but boxes waiting for the movers to come. I got that same choking, tight feeling in my chest. This was home. Denver was the first place I'd ever lived that even remotely felt like it. It had only been two years. Daddy had given me two years to finish my degree and then it was time to pay the family debt.

I squeezed my eyes shut, willing the phone to stop ringing. He made me keep it with me at all times. It vibrated in my back pocket.

I took a breath. I answered.

"Hey, Daddy," I said through a fake smile. I hoped it would carry over and mask my tone.

"Willow," he said, already sounding angry. "Are we going to have any trouble today?"

"No," I answered, leaning hard against the wall.

"The movers will be there later this afternoon. I want you long gone before that."

"I will be," I said, biting my bottom lip. It was true. It just wasn't what he meant.

"You're doing the right thing," he said. "For you. For all of us. It matters that you keep your word."

I meant to keep that bright, fake smile on my face and tell him the things I knew he wanted to hear. But, something broke inside of me as I tried to muster up the will to try. I was just...tired. Of all of it. Tired of trying to please my family and always failing. Tired of swimming against the current. Tired of having things dangled in front of me then taken away. It dawned on me then that coming to Denver was a huge mistake. If I hadn't, maybe it wouldn't hurt so much to leave.

"You don't have to worry about me," I said. "I can take care of myself."

My father sighed. "Willow..."

"I'm not a child," I said. "I'm twenty-three years old. I don't need you or Lisette or anyone else checking up on me."

"Then stop acting like a child," he said. "And stop acting like your life is something that it isn't. You've wanted for nothing, Willow. Trips to Europe for your gap year? You got that. You wanted college so you could take your pictures. I made that possible. You've been living rent-free in the most luxurious apartment I could get for you."

"Daddy, I'm grateful. I never asked you for any of that."

"You asked for all of it, Willow."

His voice boomed, sending a shock wave through me.

"Even Jason," he said. "He's what you wanted. I was against it at first. You know that. I thought you were too young. But, then I saw you together. You're a good match. He suits you."

I bit my tongue. I wanted to spit out the truth. It was Jason Soren's bank account and family connections that won my father over.

"I'm grateful for everything you've done," I said. "I am. It's just..."

"Stop right there," he said. "Not another word. Life is hard, sugar pie. You have no idea what I have to do to keep you and Lisette comfortable."

"I don't need you to keep me comfortable," I said. "I don't want..."

"You listen to me," he cut me off, his voice lowering to a hiss. "You are going to finish packing your things. No...the things I bought for you. Then, you're going to go downstairs and get in the car Jason arranged for you. You're going to get your ass to Virginia where you belong. You will not embarrass me or this family with any more of your antics, Willow."

I curled my fist, digging my nails into my palm. "Will you at least just let me get to Virginia on my own? I don't need some driver. I can take the bus."

I heard something shatter on the other end of the phone. He'd thrown something against the wall, no doubt. It meant Lisette, my stepmother, would come flying out of whatever room she was in. She would fawn over my father and call me later to guilt trip me.

Lisette was a master manipulator. She'd been pulling my father's strings for fifteen years. He'd been vulnerable back then, just after my real mother's accident. It left her in a coma for months. Now, she was in a nursing home, trapped in her own failing mind. I grew misty-eyed as I always did when I thought about her. She died that day when I was just six years old. Her body just hadn't caught up. Every once in a while, if she was having a very good day, she would smile when I came to visit. My face seemed familiar, and a tear would come to her eye. But it never took long before she slipped away.

I hated this. I hated that even having this conversation made me feel like the spoiled brat my father painted me as.

My father smothered me with his attention and his money and his family commitments. I couldn't escape them if I tried. Everyone on the planet knew who Daniel Rousseau was or who he was connected to. The Family. My uncle Adam was head of one of the most influential crime families in the country. Neither of them thought I knew. They thought I really was the spoiled, naive little girl they tried to raise.

The irony was, Jason Soren was a symptom of all of that too. As my father railed on the other end of the phone, I pictured Jason in my mind.

He was tall, darkly handsome with hooded amber eyes and long legs. I met him when I was just fourteen years old. He seemed so different than my father. Calm. Quiet. Refined. And he was the only man I'd ever seen unafraid to challenge my father and more shocking still, my uncle Adam.

I fell in love with him. Hard. He seemed like some dark knight in shining armor who could pull me away from the Family. He could, I knew. But I wasn't some teenager anymore. My father had drilled into my head for years that I wasn't capable of making it without the family help. I didn't believe that anymore. I finally understood my own mind.

Except, now it was too late.

I was eighteen years old when Jason Soren asked me to marry him. I said yes. And I kept saying yes. Only now, I felt like I couldn't breathe.

"Willow," my father said, calmer. No doubt Lisette had gotten a hold of him. She was probably standing behind him, rubbing his shoulders, holding his gin and tonic in her waiting hand.

"Baby doll," he said. "Did I tell you how excited Lisette is to see you next week? She's attended to every detail. The wedding is going to be a smash hit. You'll be in every magazine."

Magazine? Lord, he sounded a hundred years old.

"Daddy, I just...I just need a minute. That's all. Can you understand that?"

He was talking through gritted teeth. "It's normal to get cold feet, honey. It's nothing to worry about. Everything is going to be spectacular. You don't have to worry. Jason will take care of you."

Ugh. I didn't want to be taken care of. Why could no one see that? There was an edge to his voice. A deeper meaning he didn't think I understood. My father wasn't happy for me about marrying Jason Soren. He was happy for himself. I knew how close he was to losing everything. Bad advice, bad investments, and my uncle Adam's paranoia had all but ruined my father in the last year. Lisette took me into her confidence and laid it all out. My marriage to Jason was the only prospect my father had.

It wasn't fair. It was positively medieval. But for now, it was my reality.

I wasn't kidding. I really couldn't breathe. Black spots swam in front of my eyes as my father kept talking about guest lists and press, and pride.

"Daddy," I said. "I need to hang up now. The movers will be here soon and I have a few things left to box."

"All right, Willow," he relented. "I expect a call from you within the hour though. Just to tell me you're on your way."

I didn't answer. He just kept on talking as though I had. Then, my father finally clicked off, leaving me shaking as I stared at the phone screen.

In another few minutes, Lisette would call. She'd take a softer, more passive-aggressive tone. She would tell me how my father wasn't sleeping anymore. How betrayed he felt by his brother. How she knew in her heart he couldn't take one more family member turning against him.

I was wrong though. My phone rang again, but it wasn't Lisette. Jason's number came up. My heart froze. I was far less able to mask my emotions with him. He knew me too well.

I just needed that minute. A day at most. Maybe I could muster up the courage to ask for more time. Jason and I had been engaged for over five years. We'd put the wedding off two years ago so I could finish up my visual arts degree. Jason was in no rush. He loved me. But, he understood my reticence better than my father did.

I let the phone go to voicemail. I couldn't help but feel my father had put him up to calling, unsatisfied with the things I said. It made me resent Jason just a little bit more.

They would all hate me. I knew this. Sure, it might seem like the easy thing to do was simply come clean. I wasn't ready. I wasn't sure. I needed time. Only, I'd been down this road so many times before. My father would overreact. He would track me down. Once, he sent men to pull me out of class when I ignored his calls for a day. Another time, he had me followed to and from work for a week after Jason and I got in a fight. He talked about giving me the freedom to travel Europe when I was nineteen years old. There had been nothing free about it. He sent two bodyguards to shadow me 24/7.

Not this time. I couldn't take it. My chest grew heavier. Sweat broke out on my brow.

I looked around the now almost empty apartment. My furniture was gone. Sold. Packed away. Everything I really needed—my wallet, passport, a few changes of clothes—I had stuffed into my canvas backpack.

I set my cellphone down on the counter. I wouldn't need that either. Tomorrow morning, I'd call my father from a pay phone if I could find one. Or I would pick up one of those prepaid phones from the grocery store. One week. I just needed one week to disappear and clear my head. Then, I would do what I had always done. I would take care of my family.

The phone rang again. Jason. I wondered if he would call

my father next if I didn't answer. Either way, I knew Daddy tracked me from that phone. There had been far too many coincidences over the years where his underlings would show up no matter where I was.

I tucked my hair under my favorite knit cap, took one last look at my empty apartment, and headed out the door.

I gave Dreyfus, the doorman, a smile as I slipped through the revolving doors leading to the street. He tipped his hat and waved. With any luck, Dreyfus wasn't on Daddy's payroll.

The crisp, spring air hit my face as I adjusted my pack, looked both ways, then headed down the street.

I planned it all out. I was just four blocks from the nearest bus stop. I'd go to Flagstaff, or Vegas, or maybe all the way to the ocean. It didn't matter. For a few days, I just needed to disappear.

My heart soared with each new step. This was right. I could apologize later. If I didn't cut loose now, maybe I never would.

The bus stop was only one more block away. I could see people beginning to gather near the covered bench. I would blend in, become faceless. Nameless. Free.

The bus rounded the corner. People on the bench stood up and formed a line. I was almost there.

Then, a shadow fell across the sidewalk behind me and I

knew. The bus came to a halt and the hydraulic doors hissed open.

"Miss Rousseau?" His voice was deep, commanding. My heart turned to ash. I could run, but it would do no good.

I froze. I turned. He was huge, of course, with a dark, brooding face. A wall of a man with a broad chest and hard-cut muscles beneath his impeccable suit.

"Miss Rousseau?" he said again.

I forced a smile. He froze just like I did. He seemed a little shocked to see me. Was I not what he had expected? Because he was exactly who I knew would always come.

"Well," I said. "You planning on just standing there, or are you gonna throw me over your shoulder and give me a spanking?"

It was so subtle, I almost didn't see it. But, a fire lit inside of me as I watched the change go through his eyes. They were blue, but I swear they glinted like sapphires for a moment. Then, he recovered and reached for me as the bus doors closed and the driver pulled away.

CHAPTER THREE

Val

She was planning to run. It was written all over her. The backpack, the eff-you eyes with her hand on her hip. She was trying to play it off, but I could tell it mattered to her when the bus pulled away from the curb.

Shit.

Something was definitely off about this girl. She seemed to be doing everything in her power to blend in, to look like something other than the spoiled rich girl she had to be.

"My name is Val," I said. She looked me up and down. Mostly up. I towered over her by nearly a foot. She was skinny. Fine-boned with tiny wrists and small feet. She had a chest on her though. I tried not to be obvious about looking. Her t-shirt stretched tight over her breasts and came to a vee. She had on a beat-up leather bomber jacket that she probably paid hundreds of dollars for so that it looked worn and old like the real thing. Hipster chic.

The wind lifted her long hair. I wanted to take off my jacket and put it around her. I wanted to taste her.

"Val," she said, tilting her head to the said. "You sound Russian."

"I am," I said. My accent was still there after twenty years. People told me it got thicker when I was pissed off.

"So," she said. "What are my orders? What's my father got you doing for him?"

"Your father?" I said. "I don't work for your father. I was sent here to make sure you got where you needed to go."

She blinked rapidly. Her eyes were a cool green with flecks of gold when the sun caught them.

"So then who sent you?"

I looked across the street. In a few minutes, there would be another bus. I didn't like the crowd starting to gather. A couple down the block was staring straight at Willow. It got my back up. We were too out in the open.

"Come on," I said. "We've got a long drive ahead. I'm sure you have a suitcase or something."

She adjusted her backpack. It was a bug out bag if ever I'd seen one. What the hell wasn't Payne telling me? Or worse yet, was there something Soren had left out about her? I needed to know her story, and fast. If she was planning on meeting someone, it would make a huge difference in how this job went.

"Sure," she said. Her skin had gone a little paler. This whole sassy, zero fucks attitude didn't feel right. It was a front. I could sense it in the way her eyes flickered and the tiny pulse she had beating furiously in her throat. She was scared of something. I hoped it wasn't me.

She gave me a half-assed salute and started walking back toward the apartment building. The bellman had his back to us. As we approached he turned. His smile dropped for a fraction of a second, then he plastered it back in place.

"Good afternoon, Miss Rousseau," he said.

Willow walked in front of me. I couldn't see for sure what she did, but her body language was unmistakable. She'd just flipped him off. She didn't miss a trick. No doubt she put together that he'd been the one to tell me which way she went.

Willow was silent as we rode up in the elevator to the penthouse suite. She pressed a code into the keypad and in we went.

Her apartment was actually smaller than I expected. Just two rooms. A great room with a kitchen and living space overlooking the street below, then one bedroom in the north corner. All the furniture had already been hauled away. She had boxes stacked against one wall. There were just two pieces of luggage near the kitchen counter. Had she been planning to chuck those and just take off with whatever she had in her pack? I needed to get Payne on the phone quickly. I was pretty damn sure nobody had told Willow Rousseau I was coming.

"Just those," she said, sighing and pointing to the luggage.

"Got it," I said. "You can call the bellman to send someone for them."

She raised a brow. "What's wrong with you?"

I straightened my jacket. "Not part of my job description."

She shifted her weight from one leg to the other. "Isn't that what my father's paying you for?"

"I told you, I don't work for your father. My firm was hired by Mr. Soren to make sure nothing happens to you."

"Soren," she said, her face falling. "Jason hired you?"

It seemed to genuinely scare her. Dammit. I felt like I was flying blind here. We were off on the wrong foot in so many different ways.

"Apparently," I said. "I'm driving you to Virginia."

There was that rapid blinking again. If I had to guess, she looked like she was holding back tears. What the actual hell was going on? This chick went from haughty princess to scared shitless in a heartbeat. I wanted to go to her. I had an overwhelming urge to put an arm around her and pull her close. Even that was out of character for me. I didn't know her. She was just a job. But then, my focus kept going to that fluttering pulse near her throat. Her heart was beating a mile a minute. Tiny beads of sweat broke out on her brow.

"Listen," I said, taking a softer tone. "I'm not here to get into your personal business..."

"Aren't you?" she said, her voice cracking. She seemed pissed and scared all at once again.

"No," I said. "I'm here to keep you safe. That's all. It's my understanding there have been some...threats."

I had to be careful. Was it possible she was oblivious? Payne's report detailed a kidnapping attempt two months ago. Willow was apparently at a club downtown when two men came after her in the parking lot. I'd read the cold facts on paper just a few hours ago. Now, as I stood in front of her, the image of her that close to danger stirred my wolf. Hard.

I became aware of her scent. Delicious. Sweet. It heated my blood. I shuddered. I cleared my throat and forced myself to focus. This girl was a mystery. And worse, being near her raised all sorts of questions. Questions I would need Payne to provide answers to. But, in the meantime, my job was clear. I would get her to Virginia in one piece.

"Threats," she said. "I've been threatened my whole life, Mr...Val. You didn't tell me your last name."

"Kalenkov," I answered. I watched her closely to gauge any recognition in her eyes. Her family was human, that I knew. So was she. Surely Jason Soren knew he was dealing with wolf shifters when he hired us. But, I couldn't tell for sure if Willow knew what I was.

"Kalenkov," she repeated it. "That's a mouthful."

"So just call me Val. Short for Valentin."

"Valentin Kalenkov." She drew out the syllables in my name. I loved watching her lips move. They were full, bee-stung. Her tongue darted out as she licked them. Shit.

"Val," she said again. "So what, do you have some file on me? What did Jason tell you about me?"

"Mr. Soren is concerned with keeping you safe. Are you in the habit of getting yourself into trouble?"

It came out wrong, almost like a double entendre. Her face hardened.

"I'm in the habit of taking care of myself, Mr. Kalenkov. Despite what you may have heard, I don't need a babysitter."

This got a laugh out of me. I'd said the exact same to Leo no less than an hour ago. And here I was, about to argue the point with her. I stopped myself.

"We should get on the road," I said. "We're already almost two hours behind. If you'll excuse me for a second, I need to make a quick call. It'll give you a chance to pack whatever else it is you need. I'll be right outside that door."

She understood my meaning. I'd already done a quick scan. There was just the one way out unless the girl was planning to launch herself off the tenth-floor balcony. No sooner had I thought it before a chill went through me. She couldn't. She wouldn't. Dammit, I needed to get Payne on the phone double-quick.

Willow turned on her heel and went into the bedroom. I went into the hall and shut the door behind me. I could still hear her though. If I closed my eyes and held my breath, I could sense her heartbeat.

Payne answered on the first ring.

"Glad you called," he said, no doubt recognizing my number. "How far out are you."

"Still in Denver," I said. "Let's just say Ms. Rousseau is running fashionably late."

"I'm not surprised. Look, I know this isn't your idea of fun. And I also know you're probably pissed at me for assigning you this. It's scut work. I know that. But, Val, you're one of the only men I trust with this. The Soren account, well, it's important."

"I get it. I'm not calling to complain. It's just...I'm already getting an odd vibe on this one." I stepped further away from the door to make doubly sure Willow couldn't listen in. I still sensed her in the bedroom. I lowered my voice. She probably couldn't hear me if she were standing right beside me. Payne could. We weren't pack, but we'd been around each other long enough now to be almost telepathic.

"She was trying to make a run for it," I said. "If I hadn't

been on it, she would have hopped a bus to who knows where. I'd bet money on the fact she had no idea I was coming. Are we sure this girl even wants to go to Virginia?"

"Son of a bitch," Payne muttered. "Soren told me she's a handful. Impulsive. He says her father's given her way too much without telling her where it comes from. Protected her. She puts herself in dangerous situations without realizing it. Daniel Rousseau can be the worst kind of moron. A dangerous one and he's got a list of enemies as long as your arm. You've read the report. Soren doesn't want the daughter knowing, but he's got it on good authority Daniel Rousseau is a marked man and probably weeks away from going up on RICO charges. He's afraid if she *does* find out, she'll freak and try to go to him. That could be dangerous for obvious reasons."

"She might walk straight into the line of fire," I said, my wolf getting restless once more. "Still, is it the best idea to keep her in the dark? I don't think she's stupid Payne."

He sighed on the other end of the phone. "Just...can you get her to Virginia? Then she can be Jason Soren's problem. I can't say I one hundred percent agree with his thinking, but I'm certain the guy's in love with her. Just...get her there."

"Got it," I said, still not entirely satisfied. "Get her to the church on time. That's the gig?"

"Pretty much," Payne answered. I felt ash in my mouth. I got an image of Willow Rousseau, her auburn hair flowing and those perfect, round breasts bursting out of a tight, silk wedding dress. I shook my head to clear it. This was no good. I'd been in the field way too damn long.

"I know I can count on you, Val. Just keep your eyes open and your senses sharp. Jason Soren doesn't strike me as an alarmist. If he thinks his fiancée could get in her own way on this, I believe him. She matters to him. So, she matters to us."

"Got it," I said, though I was starting to hate it. I really wanted to get in a room with Jason Soren myself so I could read him.

"Good man," Payne said. "I'll see you when you get back to the Louisville office in a few days. We've got a lot to talk about."

"We do," I answered and clicked off. The apartment door opened and Willow stood there, her cheeks flushed, her breasts heaving. She projected calm, but I knew she was anything but. Hell, it was the same for me.

"Well," she said. "If you're in such a hurry, what are you still doing standing there?"

I had the urge to take her up on her earlier suggestion and bend her over for a spanking. Just the thought of it made my blood sing. My vision went foggy and I quickly shielded my eyes. If she had been looking straight at me, she would have seen my wolf eyes flash silver.

CHAPTER FOUR

WILLOW

Valentin Kalenkov. Of course they would send a Russian musclehead to make sure I did what I was told. Val stood in the doorway, his hands folded in front of him. He was big. Formidable with deep, penetrating blue eyes. I made a joke daring him to throw me over his shoulder. The thing was, he could have. In a heartbeat.

That should have terrified me. In a way, it did. I was fast on my feet, but if this guy wanted to get in my way, I was done for. I'd have to outsmart him.

My phone was still on the kitchen counter. I prayed neither my father nor Jason would text. If I could get the hell out of here and leave it behind, then at least Daddy couldn't track me that way. He thought I hadn't figured out he installed the GPS app like I was some twelve-year-old. There had just been too many coincidences over the last few months.

"Let's just get out of here," I said. "Traffic on I-70 will be a bitch as it is."

"That's why we should have left almost two hours ago," he said, his voice had a rich, deep timbre that sent tiny vibrations up my spine.

"Sorry," I said and half meant it. I knew what he thought of me. I knew what everyone thought of me. Daniel Rousseau's spoiled little mafia princess. I came all the way to Denver for a chance at a fair shake at school. I didn't want any special favors. I wanted to be judged on whatever true talent I had as a photographer. If I failed, then I failed.

Except I didn't.

Last month, my work was featured in a student showcase. I sold every last piece. One of my professors had recommended me for an internship in New York with an artist I admired. When I mentioned it to my father, he threatened to cut me off.

Five years ago, if he had said something like that, it would have terrified me. Now, it thrilled me. God. Maybe he was right. He said I could never commit to anything because I had the luxury of his money and influence propping me up.

Val held the elevator door open for me. He ushered me inside, his face hard and stoic. Still, he had a glint in his blue eyes that sparked my heart. It had to be that edge of fear again. And simmering rage. He tried to tell me Jason had sent him, but I knew better.

I held my breath as the elevator door shut and we began our descent. My cellphone never beeped. It was still on the kitchen counter as the elevator doors opened and we stepped out into the lobby.

"This way," Val said. He pointed to a sleek, black SUV across the street. He tapped his key fob and the thing roared to life. He looked both ways and put a light hand at the center of my back, guiding me across the street.

A fleeting thought made my heart trip. What if I made a run for it right here? I could scream, make a scene. Would Val try to stop me?

Panic squeezed my heart. If I got in that car with him, there might be no way of turning back. He would deliver me to Jason. I knew what would happen. Guilt would pull at me. Jason had expectations. It wasn't his fault. I hadn't been honest with him. For the last year I told myself that our planned wedding day was so far off. I'd figure out what to do about him later. Later was now, and here I was.

Here Val Kalenkov was. Was he telling the truth? Was Jason really behind bringing him here?

It got hard to breathe. All this time, I'd been trying to figure out how to deal with my father. Was Jason just a carbon copy of him?

I walked to the rear passenger seat and reached for the door handle.

"Up front," Val said.

"What?"

"I'm not a chauffeur, Ms. Rousseau. I'd rather you sit up front."

"Oh. Okay." Shit. I wasn't doing very much to disabuse this guy of an impression he had of me as an entitled brat. I wasn't sure why I cared, but I did. As Val held the door for me, I realized I cared a lot.

I thanked him as I slid in and reached for the seat belt. Val gave me a curt smile, then shut the door.

Strapped in. Trapped. I dropped my chin and tried to focus on my breathing. I was about to have a full blown panic attack right here in the car. Never mind spoiled brat, Val would think I was a nutcase.

He slipped into the driver's seat and pulled into traffic. I watched my apartment building grow smaller from the side mirror.

We sat in more or less companionable silence for a few minutes. Val told me to put on whatever I wanted. I scrolled through the satellite radio options and chose an alt-rock station but turned the volume down.

He hit the highway and picked up speed. My pulse quickened right along with his acceleration. There was no going back unless I found a way.

About an hour later...that way presented itself.

It happened almost three hours later a few miles from the

Kansas line. Val stopped for gas.

"Do you want anything from inside?" he asked. They were the first words he'd spoken to me since we hit the highway out of Denver.

"No," I said. "But, I'd like to use the restroom."

He canted his head to the side. A smile played at the corners of his mouth. He really was good-looking in a sort of brooding Alpha male way. Under different circumstances, I could appreciate having him looking out for me. For now though, I couldn't see him as much more than a prison guard.

"Ms. Rousseau," he said. "You don't have to ask me for permission to go to the bathroom. I don't know what you think I'm here for."

"Thanks," I said, feeling a little embarrassed. I slipped out of the car and we walked into the service station together.

It was one of those deluxe ones with three fast food restaurants joined by a giant food court. Val went to the cashier to pay for the gas. The restrooms were straight ahead.

He was quiet, unobtrusive except for his size, but I recognized his posture and followed his gaze. Val was scanning the area. He probably made a mental catalog of every person in the place. I half-wondered if he had some internal computer behind his eyes like a movie cyborg. He had a definite Terminator vibe to him. I knew I didn't want to get on his bad side.

Satisfied, he nodded toward the bathrooms. "I'll meet you back at the car in a few minutes. Take your time," he said.

He made cheery conversation with the clerk behind the counter. She was just a pretty teenager with dyed black hair. Her jaw dropped and she stopped chewing her gum when Val approached. She looked up and up at him.

He was still chatting with her when I came out of the bathroom. For some reason, it got my back up. He wasn't doing anything inappropriate. He just asked her a few questions about the town. Behind me, two other women came out of the bathroom.

"We can make the four-fifteen train to San Diego," one of them said. "We need to hustle. The closest station's in Garden City."

San Diego. Garden City. I don't know what stirred in me. The two ladies held a road map out in front of them. The older one traced a line on it. They wore matching fanny packs. Old friends. Partner, maybe. They might have been on vacation, but something told me they weren't. They were just carefree and on the road. My heart ached with jealousy.

There was a commotion to my right. Some drunk asshole was hassling the cashier at the burger joint in that wing of the service station.

He got louder, calling her a four-letter word that made my blood boil. He staggered sideways and brought down a rack of potato chips.

Another patron in line screamed. The guy took a swing at the cashier.

I didn't see Val move. He became a blur, leaping over the counter, choosing the shortest distance between two points.

The two fanny pack ladies turned toward the fracas. One put her hand over her mouth and started to pull her companion toward the exit.

I acted almost without thinking, seeing the opportunity and hating myself just a little for it.

"Will you help me?" I whispered to one of them.

Startled, she dropped her hand from her mouth and stared at me with an intense gaze.

"You okay, sweetie?"

I was almost out of time. Val had a hold of the drunk. The guy had been stupid enough to lunge at him. Val dodged the blow neatly and had him pinned against the wall.

I gestured with my chin toward the chaos. "He's...I came with him. I...I need to get out of here."

It was the truth, but they believed the lie my word implied. The older of the women, with cotton candy white hair gave me a grim, knowing nod.

"The Garden City train station," I said. "I wouldn't mind getting there too."

"Come on, honey," she said. "Then you better make

tracks."

Her companion started to say something, but quickly closed her mouth when she saw the look in her girlfriend's eye.

Val had his back to me. The drunk kept on fighting as two security guards finally brought themselves into the mix.

"Hurry," I whispered. "Please."

The women got in front of me. We walked with swift purpose out of the service station. They led me to a blue minivan. I climbed in the back.

The ladies were quick and stealthy as ninjas. The white-haired one got behind the wheel and pulled out. I was thrown hard against the door as she whipped into a turn and hit the road going almost sixty.

"Christ, Louise," her friend said as she struggled to get her seatbelt on.

"Don't you worry, honey," Louise yelled back. "We'll get you on that train or anywhere else you'd like to go."

I ducked down in the seat, afraid to look back. In another minute, Val would figure out I was gone. By then, it would be too late. My father's cellphone app would do him no damn good.

As Louise zipped past slower moving traffic, I started to feel the taste of freedom. I had no idea what I'd do when I got there, but Garden City, Kansas sounded like heaven.

CHAPTER FIVE

Val

"One more move and I'll break your arm," I said, trying hard to keep the growl out of my voice. I could barely see straight. I knew my wolf eyes were blazing to anyone close enough to see into them.

This was a bad idea. The last thing I was here to do was draw attention to myself. But, ever since I'd picked Willow up, the urge to shift burned so strong it choked my heart at times. Then, one asshole started getting handsy with the poor girl behind the counter and it was go time.

He had a knife. I felt the outline of it in his back pocket. He was on something. Drunk as hell at a minimum. When he took a swing at me, I damn near ripped his arm off.

"Glen!" The girl behind the counter had the presence of

mind to call for security. They were just a couple of rent-a-cops. One of them looked close to three hundred pounds. He came at me, red-faced, sweating with nothing more than a taser to subdue this asshole.

I closed my eyes and let out a slow breath. I had to get my wolf under control and quick. I wasn't here for this punk. I was here for Willow.

"You got this?" I said through gritted teeth over my shoulder.

"Uh, yeah," the red-faced security guard answered. He had zip ties instead of cuffs. If this little prick had shifter in him that would be a joke. He was human though. I whipped him around and grabbed him by the wrists, holding him steady while the guard applied the cuffs and took him from me.

""Thanks," the other guard said. "We'll take it from here."

"She can give a statement for your report," I said, nodding to the cashier.

Her jaw still hung open. She couldn't peel her eyes away from me. Dammit. I knew why. She'd seen. She knew what I was. Time to get the hell out of here.

I gave her a quick nod and tried to force a smile. The girl was smart enough to keep my secret. She composed herself, smoothing her hair under her little visor cap and started talking a mile a minute to the guards. She drew their attention from me so I could leave.

I walked back into the plaza lobby. Willow wasn't there. I did a quick scan of the convenience store then the other two fast food joints. No Willow.

My heart raced. It was dangerous to try so soon after I'd nearly shifted in front of thirty random people. But, I closed my eyes and focused on Willow's scent.

It acted on me like a drug. Sweet, feminine, delicious. A shudder went through me as my wolf clamored to get out. I was a hair's breadth from going feral right then and there.

Willow's scent lingered, wisping like smoke. But it grew fainter by the second.

My eyes snapped open. My vision darkened, going almost infrared. She was nowhere.

"You looking for someone, honey?" An older lady stood near the display of road maps. She had Coke-bottle glasses that magnified her eyes, giving her a praying-mantis quality. But, she gave me a kind smile as she got near me.

Something made her stop though. On some deep, instinctual level, she sensed something off about me.

"Did you see a young woman come out of there?" I asked, pointing to the ladies room. "Early twenties. Long, auburn hair. Ripped jeans. Wearing a pink knit hat?"

The woman scrunched her nose and shrugged. "Well, handsome, I was kind of watching you. That was pretty impressive over there. Got my old heart pumping. Very chivalrous of you to help that poor girl out."

"Thanks," I said. "Um...would you mind helping me out and checking if my friend is still in there?"

She smiled and coiled her finger around my bicep. She squeezed as I flexed involuntarily. Then, she made a big show of fanning herself.

"Oh, my," she said. "If I were just a few years younger. You just leave it to me."

"Thank you," I said, clearing my throat. "Willow. My friend's name is Willow."

She made a little salute and walked with surprising speed and efficiency to the ladies' room.

I focused on scenting Willow again. Something didn't feel right. Unless she was sick, she should be out here waiting for me.

A moment later, the old woman came out of the bathroom, shaking her head no.

"Sorry, dearie," she said. "The stalls are empty. I looked underneath. Your girl ditched you. She must be out of her mind. Did you check outside?"

I was already out the door, heart pounding. I scanned the parking lot. There were two cars filling up at the gas pumps. Four semis sat parked in the long term slots.

Willow's scent wafted past me. She'd come this way, recently. I raced to the trucks, desperate to latch on to her. She hadn't been here. That gave me a small ray of hope. If she'd hitched a ride with some trucker, there was no telling where she was or what kind of trouble she might find herself in.

"Son of a bitch," I muttered. I had been so stupid to let her out of my sight. What the hell had I been thinking?

I walked back toward the gas pumps. It was there I scented Willow the strongest. But, her scent was fading fast.

South. She'd headed south. I knew it in my gut and in my nose. There was no time to check whatever security cameras might have captured her leaving and with whom. No. The best weapon I had for finding her was me.

I slid behind the wheel of my SUV and rolled the windows down. I sucked in a great breath of air, letting Willow's scent fill me. A ripple of pleasure came with it. This time, I couldn't hold back the growl that ripped out of me.

Mine!

My wolf raged inside of me. The word came unbidden. The truth behind it rocked my heart.

No. There was no time to let my feral side take over. I had a job to do. The threat to Willow was real and I'd just been stupid enough to let her race toward it.

I put the car in drive and headed for the highway. The further south I drove, the stronger Willow's scent became. I knew I was on the right track. And I knew I had precious little time to catch up with her. She was moving fast. She was scared. Shit. She was scared of me.

Willow had maybe a ten-minute head start. I followed her scent as it branched off toward Garden City. The exit signs made my heart lurch. With each minute that ticked by, I realized where she was going. There was an Amtrak station in Garden City.

I gripped the steering wheel so hard the plastic began to bend. The wisest course would have been to pull over. I was at risk of shifting into my wolf right then and there.

Adrenaline coursed through my veins. With each breath, I felt Willow getting farther away from me and closer to danger. I should have called for backup. If everything Soren had told Payne were true when he hired us, it was only a matter of time before Willow's father's enemies caught up to her. God. The could be watching her right now. I hadn't sensed anyone tailing us when we left Denver. I made doubly sure before pulling in to the rest stop. But, what if I were wrong?

Ever since I laid eyes on Willow Rousseau, I felt like my brain and senses had short-circuited. She affected me. She called to my darkest nature in a way I'd never felt before. I had to figure out why. And I had to find a way to convince her I wasn't her enemy.

I flew down the highway. No Willow. I accelerated, weaving through traffic. Each car I passed, I looked for Willow. Had she left that rest stop willingly, or had someone gotten to her?

I sensed no fear in her scent as I trailed her. At least, not primal fear. She had likely left of her own choosing. But why? What in God's name was she running away from? Payne told me my job was to get her to Soren's estate in Virginia safely. I assumed the threat came from someone else. But, maybe Jason Soren was more worried Willow would try to run.

If that were true, this entire assignment was based on a lie. As soon as I knew Willow was safe, I had to talk to Payne again. I needed to know more about what we were doing here. Nothing felt right about this job at the moment.

I almost missed the turnoff to the train station. Angry drivers blared their horns as I cut through two lanes and took the exit ramp going almost eighty.

The train station parking lot was filling up with cars. I said a silent thank you we weren't in a bigger city yet. If this were Union Station, Willow would be that much harder to track. This was just a tiny little station practically in the middle of nowhere.

I pulled into a spot and barreled out. My nostrils flared. My heart pounded practically out of my chest.

She was close. Close enough I could feel her pulse thumping almost alongside mine.

Mine!

Down, wolf. Not now. I couldn't afford a single mistake. Not again. I'd already blown it letting my attention be diverted back at the rest stop. I would not make a stupid error like that again.

Over the PA, the dispatcher called out boarding for the next train to headed west. My breath left me as I sensed a shift in Willow's mood. She was nervous. Afraid. On the verge of panic.

I leaped over a turnstile. With every cell in my body, I knew where she was headed. A crowd of passengers was already boarding the westbound train. I didn't see Willow among them, but I knew she was close.

I ran down the yard, scanning the windows to the train. She was in there. I was sure of it. One of the station attendants tried to stop me.

"Sir," he said. "Can you show me your ticket?"

"I'm not here to board," I said, my voice more animal than man. "There's a woman on that train who may be in danger."

The attendant straightened. His eyes flashed. He looked me up and down. I pulled out my ID and showed it to him. There was something about the way he looked at me that told me he was an ally.

Then, I understood why. I sensed his animal. A jaguar. He glanced at my card and nodded. The Wolfguard Inc. logo meant something to him.

"Be quick, man," he said. "I could lose my job."

"You won't," I said. I thanked him and slipped him a hundred dollar bill. Then, I boarded the train.

My senses heightened. My vision tunneled. Willow was just a few feet away. One more train car. I could have found my way to her blindfolded. Her scent poured over me and stirred my wolf.

It wasn't anger or fear that coiled through me as I got closer to her. It was desire.

Mine!

I tried to shake off the feeling. I had to stay focused. I wasn't here to scare her or hurt her. I was here to keep her safe. I needed her to understand that.

The door to the next train opened automatically. She was sitting against the window. Her jaw set hard. She locked eyes with me and anger flashed in hers.

I took a breath. I took a step. I sat in the empty seat beside her.

"Willow," I started.

"How?" she said. She turned to me. Her eyes glistened with tears. It was like a knife in the gut. "How the hell did you find me?"

I didn't know what to say. I just knew I didn't want to lie to her. Not ever. Her trust meant everything to me at that moment. She was terrified.

"I'm not your enemy," I said. "I was sent here to keep you

safe. I can't do that if you don't tell me what's going on. What are you running from?"

Her tears fell. She looked out the window again. The conductor called out a warning. We'd be pulling away from the station in a few more minutes.

"You know someone tried to kidnap you," I said, keeping my voice low. "You know what your father does for a living."

She let out a breath. She had turned back to me, and it caressed my arm like a whisper. It stirred more than my wolf. I had the strongest desire to take this woman in my arms. I knew I would protect her with my life and it was more than just a paycheck.

"Will you come with me?" I said. "We'll go somewhere else. For lunch, maybe. I need you to tell me what you're running from."

"You work for my father," she snapped.

"No," I answered. "I told you. My firm works for Jason Soren. He cares a lot about you. Enough to pay my employer to make sure nothing happens to you."

The words burned in my mouth. Willow was a client. I couldn't afford to have anything but professional feelings toward her. And yet, I also knew this was out of my control. Something was happening to me on a cellular level when I was around her. I tried to brush those thoughts aside. If she suspected...if she knew...

"Let's just talk," I said. "That's all. I don't care who's paying me, my job is to protect you. That's what I'll do. On my life, I swear it. But, I can't fully do that if I don't know what's wrong. Will you trust me? Give me an hour."

She searched my face. I couldn't read her mind, but I felt strongly that she was about to ask me what I'd do if she said no.

She didn't. Her cheeks flushed. Her tears dried. I couldn't be sure, but I sensed something changing in her just like it had in me as she looked in me.

"Come on," I said, rising. I held out my hand to her. "A talk. That's all I'm asking. After that..."

"You'll let me go?" she asked. It gutted me. She had the wrong idea about what I was and at that moment, nothing mattered more to me than her knowing she could trust me.

"And I'll listen," I said. "I swear it on my life."

She didn't know me. A day ago, I didn't even know her name. Now, I felt my world shifting on its axis as she slowly rose and took my offered hand.

With that one gesture, she'd given me the greatest gift of all. Her trust. I knew in my heart I would spend the rest of my life earning it.

CHAPTER SIX

WILLOW

Val was so strong, so sure. His hand warmed mine and as I looked into his pure, blue eyes, something happened inside of me. I could feel my heartbeat slowing, my nerves settling. One touch from him felt like instant Xanax.

Maybe I was just looking for something solid to latch on to. He was definitely that. As we walked down the aisle toward the exit, I caught every female passenger staring at Val, most of the men too.

I wanted so hard to trust him. I never felt more alone in the world. There was no one on my side. No one. It was just me.

Val was something to behold with his towering height and well-defined muscles beneath his crisp, black suit. Something about it didn't seem right. Almost as if he were too rugged, too wild to wear something so conservative. We stepped out onto the platform. One of the station attendants held the door for us. He gave Val a knowing look that sent heat flashing through me. I wondered if he'd paid the guy off to let him on the train. Probably. It's what I would have done.

"Come on," Val said. "We don't have to hurry. My car's this way. We can just sit and talk for a while."

Talk. Now that I'd agreed to go with him, I had no earthly idea what I'd say.

The SUV was parked out front. I saw my reflection in the gleaming, black paint. I looked...small...scared. I stiffened my back. I hated feeling so vulnerable.

Val held the passenger side door open for me. I thanked him and climbed in, tossing my backpack to the back seat.

He got in and started the car, but didn't take it out of park. He turned to me.

"So, what's going on?" he asked.

I opened my mouth to answer, but realized I had far too many questions of my own.

"How did you find me?" It all sort of slammed into my brain at once. My cellphone was still sitting on the kitchen counter of my old apartment. Whatever tracking app my father had on it would have done Val no good. And yet, within ten minutes of my getting on that train, there he was. That feeling of panic and unease started to return. I couldn't breathe. My pulse quickened. I needed air. I wanted to get out.

"Willow," he said, his voice thick and deep. He gripped the steering wheel. A tiny vein jumped near his temple. He looked like he was having trouble with his own rush of adrenaline.

"Willow," he said again. "I said it once. I'll say it a thousand times. You don't have to be afraid of me. I'll protect you with my life if that's what it takes."

"What if I just want to get away from you? From all of you? You don't feel like my protector, Val. You feel like my jailer."

"I'm not," he snapped. "I swear to you. I'm not. But you're scared out of your mind. It's pouring off of you."

He barely got the last sentence out. It was almost as if my heightened state was affecting his. My heart raced. Val took a deep breath.

"I'm going to need you to calm down," he said. On some deeper level, I knew he meant it literally. *He* needed me to calm down. So he could.

I closed my eyes and exhaled. I ran a hand through my hair. A moment later, I did feel calmer. Val released his grip on the steering wheel and turned to me. "Tell me what you're really running from," he said.

How the hell could I? He told me time and again that he

worked for Jason. If that were true, he was probably duty bound to tell him everything I said.

"This is just us," Val said, as if he could read my mind. "Whatever you tell me doesn't leave this car unless it's a safety risk. Deal?"

I had to be out of my mind. He was so convincing with those piercing eyes. He stared at me with such intensity, as if I were the only other person in the world.

"I know what you must think of me," I said.

"And I promise you, you don't."

I sighed. "It's not easy being Danny Rousseau's kid. If anybody else heard me say that, they'd roll their eyes. I've had everything. It's true. Fancy houses, traveled all around the world. Luxury cars when my friends were driving clunkers. Private schools. No such thing as student loans in my world. I mean, what could I possibly have to bitch about?"

"Nobody's life is perfect," he said. "And I know something about the weight of family expectations."

"Right," I said. "But it comes with a price. I can never know whether someone is real with me. Not ever. I mean a little, at first. Until they know who my father is. Half of them just disengage completely. The other half usually want something from me. But even those people, I can see the fear in their eyes. Like oh, better not cross Willow or she'll sic her father's thugs on you. Or they assume I'm there because of some string Daddy pulled. A lot of the time, they're right. But...I've never just been able to relate to someone out of something pure. They're either afraid of my father...or on his payroll."

My throat grew thick. A bit of the color drained from Val's face. He knew he was no exception, no matter who signed his check.

"I thought Jason was a way out," I said. Now that I'd started, the words just tumbled out of me like water from a faucet. I knew in the back of my mind I should stop. I'd said too much. No matter how good Val was at pretending to care, I could never forget why he was here.

"I've known Jason Soren since I was fourteen years old. He was nice to me. And he was the first person I knew who didn't have to be. His family is even more powerful than mine. I was just some pesky kid who probably annoyed him more than anything else. Then...I wasn't. He lived in Prague for a while. For years, actually. Just after I turned eighteen, he came back home. We started talking. Eventually, he asked me to marry him and it felt like a fairytale. He knew all the right things to say. I told him *everything* and he listened. So, I said yes, but only if I could go build a life for myself first."

"So you went to college? Why Denver?"

"They have an arts program and a community that appealed to me. I first picked up a camera when I was like seven years old. I can...it lets me see the world through other people's eyes, or at least a different version than my own. I've been happy in Denver. Happier than..."

"Will you show me?" he asked. "I mean...I assume you keep a camera in that backpack of yours."

My heart fluttered with heat again. I swear I saw it go through him too. I couldn't explain it, much less understand it, but I knew in my core my moods seemed to impact his. It was empathy. Or he was the most brilliant actor on the planet.

I reached over the seat and grabbed my backpack. I pulled out the little Nikon I used on the fly. I turned it on and handed it to Val, flipping open the viewer.

I showed him how to scroll through the images. He went silent as he looked.

"They're unfinished," I said. "It's just what I've been working on."

I had the idea for a series last month. I'd been taking pictures of the same couple in the park. They were man and wife. The woman was in the advanced stages of Parkinson's. She needed a wheelchair most days. But, she loved watching the little kids play on the jungle gym while her husband sat beside her. There was joy in her face, but always worry in his. They held hands and touched in a million tiny little ways.

"These are amazing, Willow."

I got self-conscious. Val sensed it and snapped the camera closed. Smiling, he handed it back to me.

"Have you shown any of these?"

"Not those," I said. "Like I said, they aren't finished yet. But, I did have a gallery showing a while back. The owner thinks I have real promise."

"I'm not an expert, but I'd say they're right."

It made me like him a little more. And it felt like one more way he managed to dial in to me. I found it unsettling and strangely familiar all at once.

"You don't want to marry Jason Soren," he said. His tone seemed authoritative. Was it a question or a command? Whatever it was, something hard lit behind his eyes when he said it.

"I don't..." I had to be careful. I'd not given voice to my doubts to anyone yet. I knew what it meant. If I backed out on Jason, it could spell disaster for our families and embarrassment for my father. He was already on shaky ground with his associates and my uncle.

"I don't know," I said. "Maybe. I did. I was sure of it. Jason's always been a friend to me. I've never felt pressured. We've taken time to get to know each other, but it's been mostly through old-fashioned letter writing and texts. I haven't actually seen him in almost two years."

"Then it sounds like you have a lot to talk about," Val said. There was no pleasure in his voice.

"I just need a minute to breathe, you know? So I can figure out if this is really what I want."

"Reasonable," Val said. "Except, I don't understand the running. You're obviously a smart girl, and talented. And you *know* your father has enemies that would use you to hurt him. Why put yourself in that position? It seems...well...childish. Naive, at least. And I'm not trying to make you angry. I just get the impression people are in the habit of not telling you the whole truth."

He took my breath away. He was right. Nobody had ever been so blunt with me before. They were too afraid of getting on my bad side because of who my father was. I found it weirdly refreshing and infuriating.

"I'm not a child."

"I said you're acting like one. Those are two different things. You've got me chasing all over the state for you. You've made Jason Soren feel like he has to have someone like me to protect you. You've got to take responsibilities for your own choices, Willow."

"How dare you?" I said, anger rising. "You don't even know me."

"I know you were willing to take off and leave me behind to clean up your mess. You don't know me very well yet either. But, I've been straight with you. If you want some time to think or to make some different choices for yourself, there are better ways to do that besides scaring the hell out of your father and fiancé and sending me running after you. That is...unless you just like the attention."

"Go to hell," I said. I grabbed my backpack and grabbed the door handle. I pulled it frantically.

"You're a liar," I said, my voice rising to hysterics. "You're my jailer, Val. Nothing but a hired gun."

Val stayed calm, stoic. Only the tiniest smirk lifted the corner of his mouth. He raised his index finger and lowered it in a wide arc. He pressed the button to release the door locks.

"Well," he said. "You can run. I'm not being paid to kidnap you. That's your choice. Or, you could let me drive you to the Bay like I'm supposed to. And you can talk to Jason Soren face to face. Tell him how you feel. Like a grownup. If he really loves and cares about you, he'll understand. Even if he's not happy, he'll understand. If he doesn't...well...I guess that's valuable information to have."

"That's what I'm afraid of. He could hate me for this."

"He'll hate you for sure if you run. You know what the right thing to do is."

Tears played at the corner of my eyes. "But, what if he..."

Val reached for me. He wiped away my tear. His touch electrified me. I gasped from it. His eyes glinted as he drew away.

"You may have made Jason Soren a promise, but I made one to you. I intend to honor it."

"What do you mean?"

"Go to him. Tell him you want more time or that you're not ready to get married yet. If he loves you, it will be fine. If he doesn't and it's not...well...I'll be there."

"Are you serious? You work for him."

His face darkened. "My job is to protect you. No matter who I work for, that won't change. I told you, you have my word. I'll have your back, Willow. I swear it."

At that moment, nothing mattered to me more. I knew he meant what he said. For the first time in days, I felt like I could breathe again. I felt like I had a workable plan.

"Okay," I said. "We'll go to Virginia and I'll talk to Jason face to face. And...you'll stay."

"On my life," he crossed his heart with his index finger. "But no more running."

I crossed my heart like he did. "No more running."

Val gave me a devastating smile, then he put the car in reverse and we pulled away from the train station.

CHAPTER SEVEN

Val

W illow was easier with me after that. Her entire posture changed as the miles and hours ticked by and we made our way east. We stopped just outside of Evansville so she could get some sleep. I couldn't. I found a clean, little motel just off the highway and checked into the room next to hers.

In the quiet, I could feel her practically rhythmic breathing through the wall. I closed my eyes and put my hand over my heart.

I wanted her. That could be dangerous. She was scared of something I didn't understand. Whatever the real history was between her and Jason Soren, I knew I was right that she had to face it head-on. I also knew telling her that might cost me my job.

So, I called Payne.

He answered on the first ring.

"Everything okay, Val?" he asked.

"More or less," I said. I decided not to tell him Willow tried to run. I don't know why. I felt protective of her beyond the job. I was going on instinct here.

"Soren's worried," Payne said. "He says he knows she's temperamental."

"It's more than that," I said. "I don't think she's sure whether she wants to marry the guy."

"Well, that part's not our business. Just get her home in one piece. We're not in the matchmaking game."

I had to take a pause to keep the wolf out of my voice. Instinct. That was the problem. My instinct was telling me to put the girl in the car and drive as fast and far away from Virginia as I could go. Except I'd been the one who just convinced her to get off that train and head straight for Jason Soren's arms.

I pulled the phone away from my face. The hair sprouted on the back of my hands. I was in danger of shifting right there in the motel room. The girl had short-circuited my brain.

"Look, Val, I know how much you hate this. I know you want to spend your time doing more important things.

Soren's got contacts I need. But, if there's something wrong, I need to know about it."

"There's nothing wrong," I said. "It's just been a long day. And it'll be a longer one tomorrow."

"Where are you?"

"Evansville," I answered.

There was a moment of silence on the other end. "If you want...bring her to the Louisville office. I'll arrange for someone else to get her the rest of the way."

"No!" I said, my voice snapping. Dammit, I needed to get this shit in check. "No. I got this."

"You sure?"

"I'm sure. It's just...I don't know. I'm getting a feeling. And if this woman doesn't want to be anywhere near Soren, I also don't think we should be in the business of forcing her into it."

"I'll trust your judgment on it," Payne said. "Just make sure you're right. And call me when you get her there. You feel anything off, you tell me. Keeping Willow Rousseau safe is your job no matter what."

I let out a breath. "Yeah. Yeah. Okay."

"Get some sleep, man," he said. "You sound like you need it. We'll talk tomorrow."

I felt better for a moment. But, when I hung up the phone

and settled into the quiet, I could only feel Willow again. So close. The craving started low in my gut. I knew I should have just gone out, found some woods, and shifted into my wolf to take the pressure off. But, I couldn't bring myself to leave Willow's side again.

The next morning we got an early start. Willow met me at the car, fresh-faced, her hair wet from her shower. I handed her a cup of coffee I grabbed from the motel lobby. She licked her lips as she took it from me and my blood heated. Her fingers brushed mine and I saw the color rise in her cheeks.

"We should make good time if we get started."

"Ready whenever you are," she said, blowing over the top of her coffee. She slid into the seat beside me.

We sat in comfortable silence as we hit the highway. As the mile markers flew by, my heart eased. Willow was animated, gesturing with her hands as we passed each little town.

"You know," she said. "I've never done this before."

"Done what?" I asked.

Her heart fluttered, but not with fear this time. She was excited.

"I don't know...just road tripped. Someday I'd like to take my time with it. See every giant ball of yarn."

I laughed.

"Route 66," she said. "I'd love to just get one of those silver bullet Airstreams and just, I don't know...go."

I raised a brow. "Jason Soren doesn't strike me as the giant ball of yarn kind of guy."

She shrugged. "You never know. I think my father was. A million years ago. When I was little, we took fun trips. Before my mother..."

Her voice trailed off. I knew a little about her family from the dossier Payne gave me. Daniel Rousseau married his second trophy wife ten or fifteen years ago. I didn't really dig into what happened to her real mother.

"I'm sorry," I said. I could sense the answer from her posture and the darkness in her eyes as she turned to me.

"She's not dead," she said. "My mother's in a nursing home. She was in a car accident when I was six. I was with her, but I don't remember it. They said I was thrown from the car and lucky to be alive. She wasn't so lucky. She suffered brain damage."

"Again, I'm sorry." I had to bite my tongue from saying the thing I really meant. I wished I'd known Willow then. I wished I could have watched over her.

"Some days she's fine, you know? Like the light is on. But most days, she's just gone. My father rarely visits her anymore. It's gotten harder for me too. I feel guilty about that. In the beginning it was really awful. Then, my father found a place for her in upstate New York. They've been wonderful with her. Brought her out of her shell at least a little. But, she's never going to come all the way back."

"That must be hard to see," I said.

"It is. But then sometimes, like I said, it's really okay."

She turned back to the window and drew into herself. I don't know why I thought it at that particular moment, but I wondered how much of that she'd shared with Jason. Then, I found myself gripping the wheel so hard it's lucky I didn't crush it.

"You're probably getting hungry," I said. We hadn't stopped for breakfast and it was heading into the lunch hour.

"There!" she said suddenly, pointing to a rusted, bent road sign. It heralded the next little town just outside of Lexington called Raintree. "We should go there!"

"Raintree?" I read. "Willow, I don't think anyone's ever been to Raintree. That's sort of the point."

"No," she said. "The sign. I mean, it's no giant ball of yarn, but we can stop for the greatest chicken tenders in the state of Kentucky. I mean, how can they really know that? Shouldn't the Colonel get that honor?"

She was joking. Her eyes were bright. She had a dimple in her left cheek when she smiled wide enough. It was the first time I noticed. It was the first time I ever had occasion to. I liked it.

"Chicken tenders?" I said.

"I mean, come on," she said. "We've passed like a hundred waffle places. I'm hungry. Let's see if Raintree's chicken tenders are worth the hype."

My own stomach growled in response. If traffic cooperated, we'd make it to Soren's place by the end of the day. We were already half a day late.

A low, rumbling growl filled my chest as the idea of Jason Soren popped in my mind again. Willow was set to marry him. She said she loved him...once. Whether she decided to go through with the match was up to her, but the thought of it woke my wolf.

Mine!

I let out a hard breath.

"Val?" she said. Willow had been talking, but her words hadn't penetrated my consciousness. A flash of jealousy went through me.

"Hey," she said. She put a hand on my wrist. "Your fingers are practically turning blue."

I had the steering wheel in a vice grip. This was no good. My principal duty here was to keep Willow safe. I sure as hell couldn't do that if I went full wolf behind the wheel right in front of her.

"Chicken tenders," I said, making a sharp turn to catch the exit. "Sounds like a slice of heaven."

Two minutes later, we pulled into Mel's Chicken Shack in

Raintree, KY. It was a sleepy little lakeside town in the literal middle of nowhere. The heavenly aroma of fried food hit my nose and I realized how hungry I really was.

"It smells like magic," Willow gasped.

"No," I said, absently, "Magic has more of an earthy smell."

Willow froze. Her face broke into a grin wide enough to show me that dimple. "You're a comedian now," she said. "Come on."

We walked into the tiny diner. It wasn't much to look at. It had rows of red vinyl booths and a u-shaped counter in the center. At first, I wasn't sure it was even open. The sign read "Seat Yourself."

I picked a booth in the far end of the room and seated myself facing the door. Willow slid in opposite me and a fast-talking old man came toddling out of the kitchen.

"One basket or two?" he asked.

"No menus?" Willow asked.

The old man took a pencil out from behind his ear and pointed to the huge sign above the counter. Here at Mel's Chicken Shack, you could order a basket of chicken tenders and that was it. The only choice was spicy or regular. Fries, coleslaw, and Coca-Cola came with everything.

"A basket of the regular recipe for me," she said.

"Two," I said.

The old man, who I had to assume was Mel, nodded and whistled back to the kitchen. "Two regulars, honey!"

"I've got ears," "Honey" hollered back. Then, Mel muttered something under his breath and went back into the kitchen. He reappeared less than a minute later carrying our heaping baskets of the best chicken tenders in Kentucky. He set them down and pulled two bottles of Coca-Cola out of his apron pocket then slapped the bill facedown between us.

It was perfect.

Willow picked up a chicken tender with her fingers and bit into it. Her face went through a series of changes. Wonder, disbelief, then ecstasy. She moaned as she took another bite.

I bit into one of my own. The sign was right. These were the best chicken tenders in Kentucky. Probably everywhere. Moist, succulent, coated with the perfect crunch and a hint of pickle juice.

"Good call," I said, waving a tender at Willow.

"I think I never want to leave this place," she said.

Her words cut through me. With aching clarity, I realized I didn't want to leave either. I wanted to spend days getting to know this woman. I liked this side of her. She let her guard down. She'd put her trust in me.

"I like you like this," I said, deciding to be at least that honest with her.

She grabbed her napkin and wiped a small spot of grease from her chin. "With a face full of chicken?"

"No," I said. "You just seem happy. I don't know you that well, but I get the impression you aren't very often. Happy, I mean."

Her face fell. She wiped her hands and put down her half-eaten chicken tender. She'd polished off three of them already. The things were about as big as a baby's arm. I'd finished my own in record time and knew I could easily dig into her leftovers.

"I'm not spoiled," she said.

"I didn't say you were."

"I have everything. I know that. My father always tells me I should be more grateful. He thinks I don't know what it's like for people who weren't born his daughter."

I tossed my napkin on top of my empty chicken tender basket. "I think maybe he doesn't know his own daughter very well. Happiness doesn't come from the things you have. At least, if it does, it's not real. Look, I suppose it's not my place to even say it. You just...ever since you made a decision back at the train station, you've been a different person."

"I haven't though," she said. "Made a decision, I mean. I don't hate Jason. I just...I just know I'm not ready to get married now. It doesn't mean I won't later. And I'm hoping he understands."

I cracked my knuckles. I could smell the wild scents coming from the lake nearby. I could go a day, maybe two. But very soon, I'd need to let my wolf out.

"You took control," I said. "That's what I mean. You don't have to be what you think your father wants."

Willow took out a fifty-dollar bill. I tried to grab the check, but she waved me off. "This was my idea," I said. "I insist."

She handed Mel the money and told him to keep the change. His eyes widened. He shot Willow a smile and disappeared back into the kitchen. We were still the only people in the restaurant.

"I know something about trying to live up to other people's expectations," I said. "I come from a family like yours. Well, not exactly like yours. But, my brother runs a powerful enterprise back home."

"Russia?" she asked.

"Yes. It was always assumed that I would stay by his side. It's a complicated story, but he saved my life when he got me out of there. Circumstances have improved, and now he's gone home."

"But you stayed," she said. "You like doing what you do?"

I nodded. "I like having the freedom to choose what I want to do. And yes. I think I'm better suited to my current employment."

"So, how does one get into the bodyguarding biz?" she asked. "What are you, former KGB?"

"How the hell old do you think I am?" I laughed.

"Sorry."

"I'm thirty-five," I said. "I've lived here, near Chicago since I was a teenager."

"Hmm," she said. "I don't know. There's just a...way about you. I thought you were former military."

"What way is that?" I bristled. Willow always seemed on the verge of figuring something out about me. I was pretty sure she wasn't aware of shifters. Not yet. But Soren had to be. The man had to know what he was getting into when he hired the firm.

"You're just...I don't know. It's like you're more in tune with things going on around you than most people. I've had friends who came back from Iraq and Afghanistan. You remind me of them."

I checked my phone, wanting to steer her attention away from me.

"Oh, I'm something all right," I said. "But right now, what I am mostly, is late. We should get back on the road if we want to make it to the Bay by the end of the day. I'm surprised Mr. Soren hasn't tried to call you."

A strange expression came over her face. All at once, it

occurred to me that I hadn't seen her on her phone since I picked her up.

"You're right," she said. "Let's get going."

She called back to Mel, complimenting him on the chicken tenders.

"Tell your friends," Mel shouted as the door chimed above us.

Willow was quieter, more pensive as we headed out. We drove in peaceful silence for hours. As the afternoon sun faded into evening, she fell asleep against the door.

It took everything in me not to pull over and watch her. She really was beautiful. It was hard to see at first. She liked to wear that knit cap pulled down so low it covered her eyebrows. It rested in her lap now and her hair fell over her shoulder.

I grew bold, reaching over to lift a strand of it between my fingers. Soft as satin, lit with bits of gold and fiery red as the fading sunlight hit it. Her full, rose-colored lips twitched in her sleep, making her dimple prominent. My wolf stirred, imagining what she could be dreaming about.

A fleeting thought hit me. Then, the force of it blew the air from my lungs. I wanted her. God. Need clutched my heart. I wanted to drink in her scent, taste her in her most sensitive parts, run my tongue along her breasts.

I nearly lost control of the car. The tires screeched as I

swerved wildly to the right. Willow jostled, but didn't wake. Panting, I righted the car and got back on the road.

I pulled up a true crime podcast. Anything to focus my mind on something other than the alluring woman sleeping beside me. The sooner I got her to Soren's house, the better it would be for both of us. Probably.

At least, that's what I told myself as the miles flew by.

Willow finally stirred. Yawning, she sat up in her seat. "Where are we?" she asked. It was full dark now.

My throat felt dry as I answered. "We're here."

Jason Soren didn't live in a house. He lived in a mansion. His family estate sprawled hundreds of acres along a private, inland lake. I drove down a mile long private, peach tree-lined drive. When we reached the inner gate, I pulled up to a speaker box.

"Ms. Rousseau has arrived," I spoke into it. My blood felt thick.

Willow sat silently beside me as the gates opened automatically.

Lights flickered from the huge, Victorian-era mansion. It had a circular drive in front. I noted a gatehouse on the way up, and stables off to the east.

It was beautiful. Perfectly manicured in every way. But, the air felt dark and oppressive just the same. Every sense in me pricked.

There was someone or something watching as I slowed the car and parked in front of the main door. I heard barking in the distance. The horses brayed. They sensed me, perhaps.

Was it magic I sensed? I couldn't be sure. Whatever it was, something didn't feel quite right.

"Come on," Willow said, smiling brightly, but her eyes held a tinge of fear.

"This was your idea," she teased. "If it were up to me, I'd be on a train to San Diego."

Nodding, I opened her car door and offered my hand as she stepped out. As the front door opened, I found myself wishing like hell we'd just stayed on the damn train.

CHAPTER EIGHT

WILLOW

Val oozed tension behind me. I felt him as a solid presence, his muscles bunched, his eyes glimmering with untapped raw power.

"Miss Rousseau." A man came to the door. I'd met him once before, years ago. His name played at the corners of my mind, but I couldn't call it forth.

"Mr. Kalenkov," he said through a tight smile. He was tall, but still a few inches shorter than Val. He extended a hand.

Something made me touch Val's upper arm. He was solid granite, his muscles coiled.

"Ramsey," the man said and recognition came. Kenneth Ramsey. He was Jason's assistant.

"Please," Ramsey said. He could sense the tension in Val

just like I could. Val gave him a solid handshake but stayed by my side like a sentry. I wanted him there, but at the same time, I worried about him finding trouble. I couldn't forget he worked for Jason. Still, his presence gave me courage for what I had to do.

"Come in," Ramsey said. "I'm sorry, we were expecting you a while ago. Mr. Soren had to leave for the evening. Some business came up he had to tend to."

"No," I said. "I'm sorry. I got a late start."

We walked into the grand foyer of Jason Soren's family home. I'd been here twice in my life. Once at about fourteen years old. It's where I first met Jason. My father let me hang out at the stables while he took a meeting with Jason's dad. Andrew Soren died two years ago, and now everything in front of me belonged to Jason alone.

Marble floors, a grand, spiral staircase with a crystal chandelier so big it would fill up my entire Denver apartment. Val's footsteps echoed through the room as Ramsey led us into a study off the foyer.

He gestured toward a sitting area with sleek, black leather furniture. A gas fire blazed in the fireplace. The walls were lined with neatly organized bookshelves. I took a seat. Val stood beside me, tall and straight.

"It'll be just a few moments," Ramsey said. "I've got something for you, Mr. Kalenkov, then I'm sure you'd like to get on your way."

"I'd like him to stay," I said. Ramsey's eyes flickered, but he kept his expression neutral. "It's been a very long drive. Again. My fault. I'm sure Jason would want to extend his hospitality. When do you expect him back?"

"Tomorrow morning," Ramsey said. "And of course, we can arrange for something. Let me call ahead."

"Thank you," I said.

I watched the muscles in Ramsey's throat contort as he swallowed. No question, Val's continued presence wasn't something he expected. For Val's part, he seemed even edgier than before. His face flushed and he clenched his jaw so tight I could hear his teeth grinding. What on earth had him so keyed up?

"Miss Rousseau," Ramsey said. "We've been concerned. I understand your father has been trying to reach you on your cellphone."

I could just bet he had. Val had been discreet about it, but I knew he'd checked in with his boss at the security firm where he worked. Though my dad couldn't track me with the phone, he had to know I was okay and on my way. This was all about control. I bristled at it.

"I'm afraid I left it back in the apartment in Denver," I said. "I've been meaning to get a new one."

Ramsey's eyes flicked from Val back to me. "Well, in any event, your family would like to hear from you."

He reached into his breast pocket and produced a note. He

stepped forward to hand it to me and Val made a low, threatening sound. It was almost a growl.

Again, I touched his arm. He settled.

I opened the folded note and my throat ran a little dry. I expected a message from my father. It was from Lisette though, my stepmother. It read, "Call me before you talk to Jason. It's important."

She left a number I didn't recognize. The whole thing was extremely out of character for her. Lisette rarely called me herself, preferring to speak to me through my father. I didn't exactly hate her. I appreciated the stabilizing influence she was on my dad. But, I'd always found her cold.

"Thank you," I said.

"You can use the landline," Ramsey said, pointing to the simple desk in the corner. "Dial eight to get an outside line."

I thanked him again.

"I'm sorry," he said. "It's so late, but can I have the cook get something for you?"

"No," I answered. "We've eaten. I'm just incredibly tired, and I assume Mr. Kalenkov is too. If you could just call up and arrange a guest room for him."

"Of course," Ramsey said. "Mr. Kalenkov, there are actually a few things I need to go over with you. Why don't you follow me and we'll go to Mr. Soren's office? Miss Rousseau can have some privacy for her phone call."

I looked up at Val. His face had gone nearly purple.

"That's a good idea," I said quickly. Val made a move and for a moment I thought he'd argue with Ramsey. He didn't though. He just gave me a curt nod and spoke so low I doubted Ramsey could even hear him.

"You call out if you need anything. I'll find you later."

His voice was deep, commanding, and sent a flutter of pleasure through me. God. I needed to have a talk with Jason and fast. The thought of *that* sent a flutter of dread through me.

I waited a moment as Ramsey took Val down the hall. When their footsteps receded, I opened Lisette's note again. It was just past ten p.m. She might not even be awake right now. Then there was the number. It wasn't Lisette's cell. It wasn't my father's landline. My curiosity more than piqued, I went to the phone.

I dialed. Just before the phone rang, I heard a clicking noise and wondered if someone might be listening in. Ever since I'd stepped foot in this house, Val's tension rubbed off on me. I was downright paranoid.

"Willow," Lisette answered, out of breath. How the hell did she already know it was me?

"What's going on, Lisette?" I asked.

"Where the hell have you been? Do you have any idea how worried your father has been?"

"You know where I've been. Jason knows where I've been. And I'm a grown woman. I don't answer to you."

She let out an exasperated breath. I could almost hear her fake smile through the phone.

"Willow, look. Why don't we both just cut the crap? You tried to take off again, didn't you?"

My cellphone. Of course my father had already figured out I'd left it.

"Again," I said. "Grown woman."

"You ungrateful little...This is so easy for you. You've never had to work hard for anything. You don't have the first clue what's going on around you."

Rage bubbled up inside of me, making my very blood sting. I took three deep breaths. Screaming at Lisette wouldn't do me any good.

"What do you want, Lisette? What's with the cryptic note? And what number even is this?"

Her words came in a rush. "I didn't want your father to know you called me. Or that we talked at all. If he found out...I made a promise, Willow. God. I've kept more secrets than you can possibly imagine. But, I'm not stupid. You think I don't see your wheels turning. You have responsibil-ities. It's time you lived up to them. It's time you understood what's really going on. Your father's wrong. He thinks keeping you in the dark is the best way to protect you. You've told me twice how grown up you are. Time for you to prove it."

My heart thumped in my chest. "What are you talking about?"

"Jason," she said. "I need you to wake up, little girl. I told you. I know you tried taking off again. It doesn't matter how. But, you're at Jason's. You wouldn't be calling me here if you weren't. I just want to make sure you aren't thinking of being selfish again. Your wedding is in two weeks. It needs to happen. Do you understand?"

It was as if all color leached out of my vision. My chest got so tight, I felt like I was choking.

"Lisette," I finally said. "What I do is up to me."

"Shut up and listen," she said, lowering her voice to a whisper. I got the distinct impression Lisette was hiding, wherever she was.

"I've *been* listening."

"You stick to the plan. You marry that man."

"Or what?" I said, my voice flat.

Lisette made a noise, almost a laugh. She was downright freaking out on me. It wasn't like her at all. Lisette was always cool and calm. My friends called her the Ice Queen.

"Your father is in trouble," she said, her voice stabbing through me. "Big, bad, trouble, Willow. You have no idea."

"So enlighten me," I said. "And what does that have to do with my marital status?"

"You selfish little..."

"You keep calling me names, I'm hanging up this phone!"

"Fine. Your father has made some enemies in his line of work. You know that. Right now, that's all he has. The Soren family is the only ally he has and it's a big one. But, if you piss Jason off. If you jerk him around, you're going to cut your father's legs right out from under him. Then, it'll be over, Willow. Do you hear what I'm telling you?"

Her words pummeled me, like birdshot.

"He'll lose everything. But, that's the least of it. The Sorens are the only people big enough to scare off your father's enemies."

"Are you saying they're going to kill him if I don't marry Jason? Lisette, you're insane. That's insane."

I heard a door shut on her end. I wondered if she was hiding in some closet.

"That would be the least of it. Willow, you're not naive. You know your father's a made man. But that won't be enough. Without the Sorens, he'll be a sitting duck. The feds will come after him. Jason has made big promises. But, he won't hesitate to break them if he has no ties to the family. You have to be that tie."

"You can't put this on me. He can't put this on me."

"You owe him, dammit! He's given you everything!"

"I don't care about the money," I said. "I never have."

She laughed. "I suppose you don't have to. But, you've never lived without it. I have. And who do you think keeps your mother living in the style to which she's grown accustomed?"

I wanted to reach through the phone and slap her.

"Your dad put your mother in the finest nursing care facility in the country. That costs money, honey. You think Medicare pays for that? Without your father's backing, your mother will be shipped off to the lowest cost state facility. Her teams of doctors. Rehab? All of it...gone. You know what that would do to her."

I did. I hated Lisette at that moment. My mother would never fully recover. But she thrived on routine.

"It'll be your fault. It'll be on your head. And your father will be in the ground if he's lucky."

"I can't believe this. You're actually telling me I have to marry Jason to keep the sky from falling down."

"On all of us," she said. "Jesus. Why can't you get over yourself for a second? Jason loves you. He's handsome. Educated. He'll be good to you. It doesn't have to be forever. Hell, divorce him in a year or two if that's what you want. But do this now. Not for me. Not even for your dad. Do it for your saintly mother if that's all you care about. Because there's no one else, sweetie. You're it."

There was a shuffling noise and I heard my father's voice in the distance.

"I have to go," Lisette said, her voice hushed.

Before I could say anything else. She hung up on me.

My pulse thundered. Sweat poured down my back. I'd never felt more trapped in my life.

CHAPTER NINE

VAL

Ramsey sweat fear. The tiny blood vessels in his neck expanded, flushing him with color. His heart probably felt close to bursting as we walked down the hall. He led me through the kitchen. Two workers busied themselves preparing food for tomorrow's breakfast. Ramsey nodded toward one of them, but they didn't look up.

I could smell their fear too. It was wild, unchecked, primal. Neither of them would meet my eyes.

My lungs burned as we went deeper into the house. It was restored, but old. Plantation-style. Ramsey took a turn I didn't expect, opening a hidden door leading to a serpentine hallway. It probably went through the entire house. Slave passages, I guessed. The house was old enough and surely had a history. It added to the oppressive mood of the entire place.

I didn't like any of this. Not one bit. I felt more sure of something than I had in my whole life. Willow didn't belong here. There was nothing good about this.

Ramsey finally led me outside. The fresh air hit me, driving away some of the sticky heat. No sooner did my shoe touch grass before that inky, black aura encircle my senses again.

Someone was watching me. I could feel their eyes, here their measured breaths. The vast, green, manicured lawn sloped down, bordered by a thick tree line. My wolf ached to run to it. There were wild things out there. I wanted to be among them.

Ramsey turned to me. Just like that, his fear seemed to leave him. Perhaps whatever lurked in the woods made him bold. They could see. They could protect him. At least, I would let him think that.

He slipped the envelope back out of his breast pocket and handed it to me. "This should more than cover your expenses," he said.

I left him holding it. "This isn't how we work," I said. "Your boss will get a bill from Wolfgard after I submit my report."

"Well," he said. "Then consider this a bonus. Mr. Soren is very thankful for your extra efforts on his behalf."

"He hired me to look after the girl, get her here safely. I decide when that job is done. For now, she wants me to stick around. Any reason she might still feel threatened?" I said. I leaned in, getting in his personal space a little.

The guy was purely human. I had no way to tell whether Soren clued him in to what I was. It didn't matter. He could sense the power coming off of me. Even now, his fight or flight response kicked in. He might not understand how he knew, but this man understood he was in the presence of an apex predator. Ancient instinct sent his heart racing. I kept my mouth clamped shut as my fangs dropped.

"What do you think you're doing here, Mr. Kalenkov?" Ramsey asked.

"My job," I answered. "I don't hop to like you do, Mr. Ramsey. I'm here until I'm satisfied Willow Rousseau doesn't need my protection anymore."

Ramsey's eyes narrowed. "Did you already fuck her?"

Pow. Snap. I felt the hair rise on my neck. My vision went almost pure red. I had Ramsey's lapels in my fists as I drove him back against the side of the house.

"Watch your mouth," I said.

Somehow, by some miracle, I kept my wolf in check.

"You're not fooling anyone," Ramsey said. "Any idiot can see the way you look at her."

"Well, I guess you're qualified to judge then," I said. I let him go. Ramsey's shoulders dropped. He smoothed his jacket.

"Listen," he said. "Whether you like it or not, we're on the same side. We work for Soren. I don't know what your angle is. You wanna hang out until Jason gets back, I'm not going to stop you. I was told to extend every hospitality. If it makes Miss Rousseau feel better to have you lurking around, I don't give a shit. I know who you are. I know your reputation. Your...associations...might be useful to the Sorens one day. If I insulted you with this, I apologize."

He waved the envelope again, then slid it back into his breast pocket.

"What's out there?" I asked, gesturing with my chin toward the woods.

"There's a path about a quarter of a mile to the east. The stables are at the end of it. A gatehouse. But, I imagine you want to spend the night in the main house. So you can keep an ear out for Miss Rousseau. She should be heading up to her rooms now. It's been a long day for both of you. I suggest you turn in."

"If it's all the same to you, I'd like to look around. It's part of my job, you understand."

Ramsey set his jaw to the side. "Of course. I expect you to keep yourself out of trouble."

It surprised me that he didn't protest more. On the other hand, he seemed willing to go out of his way to prove Soren had nothing to hide. More than anything, I wanted to get back to Willow. I damn well didn't want to let her out of my sight. But, the woods called to me. I needed to see for myself what was out there. No way in hell I was letting Willow sleep so close to what I sensed as pure danger.

I wondered if I dared shift here. The woods were dark and deep. I knew how to keep myself hidden. The instant I thought it, the urge nearly overpowered me.

"When you're through," Ramsey said, "you can let yourself back in this door. You can take the guest room at the top of the main staircase off the foyer. I trust you can find your way?"

"I can," I said. "Thank you."

Ramsey nodded. He nearly tripped over himself getting back through the door and away from me.

The moment Ramsey was out of sight, I took to the woods. I was careful to stay to the shadows so no prying eyes could see my speed if they watched through the windows. But, I moved quick as lightning. The wild, tangy scent of the earth drew me. I craved it more than any drug. It had been weeks since I let my wolf out. Now, there was no denying it.

Dead branches cracked under my feet as I found the thickest brush. Bounding over fallen logs and brambles, I followed the scent of a hidden stream, deep underground. Rabbits and smaller prey dove for cover, clearing the way for me. But, I wasn't here to hunt. Not tonight. For now, I just needed wild freedom.

I came to a clearing. An owl hooted high in one of the poplar trees. I closed my eyes and let my ears prick. My nostrils flared as I inhaled the deep, piney aroma. There were other creatures out here, but none as powerful as me.

I pulled off my jacket and tie, my pants. Stepped out of my shoes and left everything in a neat pile atop a flat stone. Then, I threw my head back and let out the howl I'd been holding in for hours.

My wolf ripped out of me. Muscles and bone reknit. My paws dug into the soft earth. Then, I was on the run. Heated blood coursed through me.

I was nowhere. I was everywhere. I ran through the thicket, dodging rotted branches, sniffing the stream deep below.

I felt alive. Whole. Free.

My paws left the ground. I ran so fast I flew. I hadn't meant to hunt. I hungered for something far different. But, I picked up the trail of a powerful stag. Had he just stayed frozen, I would have passed him. But, he ran and my primal nature took hold.

Deeper and deeper I darted through the woods. He was quick. I was quicker. He leaped across a small dip in the earth, nearly faltering. He recovered quickly, but not quickly enough.

I was on him. It was a clean, noble death. He gave his life and blood to me, feeding the wildest parts of me. The kill sated one of my deepest needs. When it was over, I came back into myself. My heart slowed as I came to another clearing.

I got my bearings again. I had nearly chased the stag out of the woods and into the main yard. Lights twinkled through the windows of Soren's mansion.

I hadn't meant to come here, to this very spot. But, instinct drew me just like it had the deer.

Willow.

I stayed in the shadows. My dark fur blended into the night. I stood rooted to the spot as Willow appeared in the window on the third floor at the corner of the house.

She paused, looking out at the woods. She looked in my direction, almost as if she could sense me. I took a slow step backward and pawed the ground.

She was stunning. She must have just stepped out of the shower. Her hair was wet and she brushed it out.

A bright moon illuminated her. Shadows danced across her cheeks. She turned. I saw her in silhouette. She wore a thin, sheer nightgown and I could clearly see the outline of her shape. She stirred me. She had high, round breasts. Her nipples peaked. She put a hand on her flat-as-a-board stomach. Her ass was perfect, just a little plump, something to grab on to.

When she turned and faced the yard, she took my breath away. With my heightened vision, I could make out the tantalizing vee between her legs.

She froze, holding her hairbrush mid-stroke. Then, she looked straight at me.

No. She couldn't see me. That would be impossible. I was camouflaged in the shadows. My dark fur blending into the earth. Still, her lips parted. Blood rushed through her. Her pulse quickened and her breath hitched, making her perfect breasts quiver.

It was too much. As much as I wanted to be in my wolf, the man inside me fought to get out. I wanted to be with her. I wanted to make her mine.

I receded into the woods and headed for the trail along the underground stream.

I slept in the woods that night, too keyed up for a normal bed. If I was right and Willow sensed me, it was better if I kept my distance until morning.

When it finally came, I collected myself. I dressed and went back across the yard. The service door was open, just like Ramsey said it would be.

The kitchen brimmed with activity, but once again, none of the staff would meet my eyes as I went by.

I followed the voices deeper in the house, though it wasn't even necessary. I could home in on Willow no matter where she was. Her scent was imprinted on me.

She sat in the dining room, sipping orange juice. She licked her lips then took a bite of a danish. A shudder went through me. Such a simple gesture, but again my lust stirred.

"Val!" she said, breathless. She wore a black, v-neck t-shirt that plunged low, showing the swell of her breasts. I clenched my fists at my sides. The urge to kiss her burned through me.

"I thought you were gone," she said.

I shook my head. "I told you I wouldn't leave until..."

"Ah, you're here." Ramsey entered the dining room. He looked Willow up and down, his eyes settling on her breasts. I wanted to rip them from his head. Ramsey pursed his lips with disapproval. Did he expect her to wear a ball gown to breakfast?

"Mr. Soren's just gotten back," he said. "He's asked that you meet with him in the study."

"She hasn't finished her breakfast," I said. "Mr. Soren can wait."

A smile played at the corner of Willow's mouth. "Uh...it's okay. I'm actually finished now. Come on. I mean...unless you're hungry..."

"I'm fine," I said. I went to Willow's side.

"Mr. Kalenkov," Ramsey said. "You can wait here. Have a cup of coffee. Mr. Soren will check in with you before he leaves for the day."

I ignored him. I wasn't about to leave Willow. My sense of danger overrode every other sense I had. There was something here. Something dark and dangerous. I knew in my heart that Willow wasn't safe.

Except, none of that should have made sense. Willow's eyes widened. I was getting careless. My vision tunneled and I knew she could see my blue wolf eyes glint.

"It's all right, Ramsey," A deep voice, thick with menace, drew my attention. I couldn't help myself from taking a step, putting Willow behind me.

She put a light hand on my shoulder.

"Val," she said. "This is Jason. Jason, this his Val. He's been...watching out for me."

She moved around me. I tried to steady my breathing. I was damn close to losing it and shifting right there at the table.

I tore my eyes from Willow. She tossed her napkin on the table and went around it.

He stood there. Jason Soren. He was tall, broad-shouldered. Clean-shaven with deep-set, brown eyes. Handsome, I supposed.

She went to him and red rage filled my heart.

Willow stood between us. She reached for Soren's hand. He was deeply tanned and his gold Rolex flashed beneath his cuff as he took her hand and brought it to his lips. Then, he looked at me. A curious smile curled the corners of his mouth.

My heart nearly ripped from my chest as his eyes flashed

gold. It was just an instant. But, I saw his wolf struggling to rise to the surface just as mine did. Then he put an arm around Willow and drew her to his side. I caught a flash of his fangs, his message clear.

I stood in the presence of another dangerous Alpha wolf, and he had just made his claim on Willow clear.

CHAPTER TEN

WILLOW

The hairs rose on the back of my neck. My skin tingled, as if it were charged with electricity. Something was different about Jason. He stood with his fists curled at his sides. So did Val. I stood in the middle of them. I could feel their coiled rage. I heard movement throughout the house. Jason had other guards, other men working for him. Instinct told me this wouldn't end well for Val if he lost his temper.

"Jason," I said, forcing a smile. "I'm so sorry we were late yesterday. It's my fault."

A muscle jumped in his jaw. He had been clenching his teeth right along with his fists. He came to me, putting a hand on my elbow. Jason brushed my cheek with his lips and Val made a low noise. It reminded me of a growl.

"I only care that you're here and you're safe," he said, though his tone was odd. He was trying to be polite. He just came off as wooden.

It hit me again how little I knew him. We'd been texting for years. He had been a sounding board for me. Always encouraging. But, so much had happened. I'd grown up. I hadn't actually been in a room with him in almost two years. It might have been a thousand. Still, Jason Soren had always been kind to me. A friend. Val was absolutely right about one thing. I owed Jason the truth. He deserved to know my mind.

But, Lisette's phone call drove a knife straight through my heart. As much as I hated it, I believed her. My father's past and business had finally caught up with him. Ever since I was a little girl but old enough to understand what he did, I knew this day might come. It wasn't fair of him or Lisette to put his safety on me. If it weren't for what Lisette said about my mother's situation, I would have hung up on her.

My heart sank, thinking about the last time I saw her. She was always happy in my company, as if in some dusty corner of her mind, she knew I was someone she was supposed to love. But, the memories were gone. She was a shell of herself. Only, I knew how bad it would be for her to have to leave the nursing care facility she was in.

God. In that moment, I could almost hate my father.

"Thank you again," Jason said to Val. "I'm sorry Willow gave you such trouble."

What?

Val still hadn't said anything. It was as if he had turned to stone.

"I'm sure you need to be on your way," Jason said. "I'll be certain to tell Payne Fallon how much I appreciate you going over and above for Willow. Her wellbeing means more to me than I can express."

"I'm right here," I said, trying to take on a joking tone. "You don't have to talk about me like I'm not here."

Jason's eyes flickered, but he kept that stony expression in place.

"You can show yourself out?" Jason asked.

"I don't mind staying," Val finally said, his accent thicker than usual.

"There's no need," Jason said. "You've done what you were paid for."

"Jason," I said. "Is there someplace we can talk in private?" It felt important to get the two of them away from each other. I didn't want Val to leave just yet. I couldn't explain it, but there was something very off about Jason. On the other hand, it really had been so long since I'd seen him face to face.

"Of course," he said. He extended a hand to shake Val's again. "I really do appreciate all you've done. I'll be happy to leave you a glowing recommendation."

They shook hands and I heard bones crunch. Tiny beads of sweat broke out on Val's forehead. What in the actual hell was wrong with these two?

"Willow," Jason said. "Let's take a walk through the garden. It's a beautiful morning."

I turned my back to him, still standing between him and Val. I leaned in, taking Val's hand I moved in for a quick hug. It was over-familiar, but felt necessary.

He spoke low and quickly, so only I could hear.

"Meet me out by the stables tonight."

My pulse quickened. A rush of unbidden desire went through me, making my knees knock together.

Smiling, I gave him a quick, secret, nod. At that moment, I only knew how important it was for me to see him again. And I also knew how dangerous this was.

Val let me go. He gave Jason a curt nod, then brushed past him heading for the front of the house.

Jason was all smiles. He really was good-looking, but in an entirely different way than Val. Val was rugged, rakish with dark features and an intense stare that heated my blood. But, Jason was just as intense in his own way. Clean-shaven, immaculate with his designer suits and lean, long muscles.

"This way," he said. He put a hand at the small of my back and led me out the French doors to the rose garden.

We walked along a cobblestone path toward a high-trellised arch. Beyond it was a little gazebo overlooking the most vibrant patch of red and yellow blossoms.

Jason gestured toward the bench. I sat, thinking he would take the space beside me. He didn't though. Instead, he stood, leaning against wooden beam supporting the roof.

"So, where was it you wanted to run off to?"

Of all the things he could have said, I hadn't expected that.

"Jason..."

He put a hand up. His pleasant facade melted. Something was wrong. Very wrong.

"Jason...we need to talk."

"No," he said. "You need to listen."

His body language was all off. He towered over me, moving in close. He hooked a finger beneath my chin and lifted. He had soft, amber eyes, but today, they seemed to have gone pure black.

My heart fluttered. I felt trapped. I couldn't breathe. Years ago and through most of my teens, I harbored a girlish crush for this man. Handsome, confident, refined. I watched him go toe to toe with my father and his associates. He was smarter than they were. I knew it even at fifteen. He gave me my first, real, stolen kiss on my eighteenth birthday, the day he asked me to marry him. For the past five years, I had thought of him as my way out. But here, at that moment, it was as if I could hear the slamming of prison bars as Jason Soren held my eyes.

"Jason..."

"I need to make myself perfectly clear, Willow. As my wife...as my fiancée...I expect you to act a certain way. I've been patient. I've looked the other way while you've acted on your worst impulses. You father never bothered to check them. I will."

This was nuts. I bolted to my feet. "What are you even talking about?"

This wasn't the same Jason who had texted me words of encouragement late at night as I geared up for my first gallery showing. Over the years, I'd told him things about my father I'd been too afraid to share with anyone else. He listened. He understood. He was a friend. For so long, I mistook that friendship for something else. I turned it into a fantasy in my head. Jason Soren, my knight in shining armor.

But, it wasn't real. It had never been real. I'd known it for a very long time now. And I had let this go way too far.

"I'm not a child," I said.

"Then stop acting like one. You embarrassed me. Acting like some runaway bride."

"We're not married!"

"Yet," he said. "But, that makes this the perfect time for you to understand what's expected of you."

Blood roared in my ears. I didn't like the way Jason was looking at me. He licked his lip. There was naked lust in his eyes. I'd never been afraid of him like I was now. But, there was something else stirring deep inside of me. I couldn't name it. Couldn't explain it. Electricity skimmed up my spine. The air grew thicker and thicker. There was something odd happening to my vision. It was as if the clouds had darkened the sky. But, when I looked up, there was nothing but clear blue and sunshine.

"I love you, Willow," he said, changing tactics. "I've waited long enough for you. I'm going to give you everything you've ever dreamed of. And, I'm the only man who can."

"What makes you think I need a man to give me anything, Jason? I don't know what's going on here. I don't know if my father's been talking to you or if you've just had one too many mimosas with breakfast. You're acting like I'm some prized pig at the fair. And I don't know what marital rules you're talking about, but you can just stop."

He moved so quickly, I didn't see it. One second, Jason was standing with one leg up on the bench. The next, he had his hands on my upper arms, pushing me against the post.

"You're mine," he said. "Bought and paid for. You'll act like it."

"What the actual hell?" I tried to jerk out of his grip, but Jason held me tight. I could no longer see the whites of his eyes. They had gone black as coal. Real fear gripped my heart. He was on something. He had to be.

"You father...your mother...what do you think will happen to them if you cross me, Willow?"

"That's not on me," I said. "My father has made his own choices. I'm going to make mine."

"Do you have any idea what he's facing?" Jason asked. "Your father has never been as smart as he thinks he is. He overestimates his own influence."

Jason finally let me go. He pulled his phone out of his jacket pocket and swiped the screen. He turned it so I could see.

It took a moment for my brain to register what my eyes were seeing. There was a man, lying in the street in a pool of his own blood. His throat was slit. His sightless eyes stared up at the sky.

I knew him.

"Tony Davis," Jason said, confirming my recognition. Davis was one of my father's business partners.

"What is this?"

"This is what happens when your father can't live up to his promises," he said.

"Did you do this? Did you have Tony killed?"

"No," he said. "Your father is responsible for that. Oh, he

didn't order it. But, your father didn't fulfill an obligation to the people he works for. They sent a message through Tony Davis. Next time, they won't be so lenient. And your father knows my family is the only thing standing between him and this same fate."

"So what, if I don't marry you, you'll kill my dad?"

Jason put the phone away. "As my wife, you'll be part of *my* family, Willow. That means something. It means everything. And it won't just be your father. You mother. Your step-mother. Maybe even you. He's in that deep, Willow. I can keep you safe. But, not if you walk away."

So there it was. A pure threat. If I married Jason, he'd handle my father's enemies. It was just as Lisette had said. Only, I didn't understand.

"I'm in love with you, Willow," he said.

"This doesn't feel like love," I said. "It feels like possession."

He licked his lips again. Before I could stop him, he held me in a crushing, demanding kiss. He was all heat, all lust. It felt like a claiming. My body rebelled. I wanted to run. At the same time, I felt that spark of electricity deep in my core. It wasn't desire. But, I had the strangest sense that something inside of me came awake for the very first time.

From deep in the woods, a sound unlike anything I'd ever heard cut through me, heating my blood once again.

It was a low, threatening growl, followed by a plaintive howl. Jason pulled away as if my skin had turned to fire.

He staggered back and shielded his eyes with his forearm.

"Go back inside," he said. "We'll talk again later. And don't you dare try anything like you did on the road. This weekend, I'm throwing an engagement party. I'm going to present you to important people. People whose influence your father desperately needs. You'll play the part you were born to play, my love."

Or else. He didn't say it, but the threat was still there. I tore away from him, adrenaline coursing through me. He felt it. God help me. He felt it. It only made his midnight black eyes darken even more.

Instinct fueled me and I ran. As I reached the French doors and vaulted into the kitchen, I had that same stifling sense that prison bars had just closed behind me.

CHAPTER ELEVEN

VAL

My wolf ripped out of me. Willow's fear struck me like an arrow through the heart. She was with him. He was dangerous.

I stayed under cover of the brush, just beyond the tree line as Willow and Jason Soren made their way to the gazebo. I could see Soren's lust pouring off of him. He was having a hard time controlling his own wolf. If he made one false move, if he harmed so much as a hair on Willow's head, I would end him.

I bared my fangs, a growl running through me in constant, low vibration. It was dangerous to let it. If there were any other shifters nearby, they would scent me in a second. Soren should have. But, he was too busy trying to maintain the balance between his primal and logical nature.

It was me. I knew it. He hadn't expected to come face to face with another Alpha wolf in his own damn dining room. It had short-circuited his instincts. Made him more feral, just like it had for me.

I had to be careful. If Soren had a pack and I made a careless move, they'd be on me in a flash. As much as it tore at my soul, the best way to keep Willow safe was to keep my distance.

His hands were on her, pressing her against the gazebo post. Fear laced her scent, making it so hard for me to see straight.

Soren became nothing but an infrared shape to me. All the cool blues and greens faded to fiery red and orange. Lust. Possession. Power. Willow was unaware of what she did to him. I felt her pulse beating alongside mine. Wild. Edged with panic. She had to stay calm. If she ran. If she tried to fight, it would set Soren off like a stick of dynamite. I was fast, but still wouldn't be able to get to her in time. Willow had no idea how her nature affected a wolf shifter like me. Or like Soren.

She was a wolf's mate. I had recognized it the moment I laid eyes on her, even if I hadn't let myself believe it. She was the job. I was trained to keep my distance. But, when I touched her for the very first time, I knew. She wasn't just any wolf's mate. She was mine.

Only Soren thought the same thing. He was different than me. Just as strong, maybe, but there was an undercurrent running through him. He was on the edge of something. I knew in my heart that under the right conditions, his could go *Tyrannous*.

A *Tyrannous Alpha* was the worst kind of shifter. A pure abomination. Fueled by anger an evil, he would exert total control over his pack and his mate. They could not eat, sleep, or shift without his permission. The most powerful *Tyrannous* could make his pack kill for him, die for him.

And right then, this asshole gripped Willow's arms so hard, he would bruise her.

I would kill him. I would enjoy it. But, even as I thought it, I knew how dangerous it was to think it. I couldn't let Soren's evil get into me. I had to stay calm. I had to find a way to get Willow away from him without bringing his entire pack, if he had one, down on our heads.

He let her go. I could see her eyes glisten as she fought back the tears. I wanted to go to her, hold her, protect her with my body. But, I also wanted to make her mine.

He knew it. Deep down, Soren knew what she was to me. It's why he danced so close to the edge right now. He saw me for the threat I was to him. Damn right. He'd have to kill me to get to her if that's what it took.

Willow turned away from Soren. From this angle, I saw his eyes flash red. He was more far gone than I thought.

Careful, I thought. Willow was too close to him. She had no idea how much danger she was in. I couldn't make it worse no matter how badly I wanted to race across that yard and take him down.

I couldn't hear what she said to him. It wasn't that I lacked the power. It was only that my own predatory rage began to drive out human words and thoughts.

She was bold. Defiant. She challenged him. Oh, God. If she took a step closer...

Soren grabbed her again. My vision went bright red, then dark. I had to keep it together. For her. For me.

I found control. When I opened my eyes again, Soren was kissing her. His grip was cruel, possessive. It was a claiming. My heart ripped down the middle. To hell with the man, I would call forth the beast. I could taste his blood in my mouth.

I couldn't stop it. A howl ripped from me. Soren heard it. He sent out a call.

Dammit. I was out of time.

But, Willow was too strong for the both of us. She kept her head and finally pulled away. Her pulse raced, but she projected calm. Then, she ran toward the house. I wanted to call to her. I wanted her to run to me. Together, we'd tear through the woods and I'd get her far from Soren's grasp.

All at once, I sensed Soren's pack. Dammit. They'd stayed hidden, but Soren's rage and mine brought them out. They patrolled at the far edges of the property on the other side of the woods. They were heading this way and fast.

I kept my eyes on Soren. He stared at the woods, searching for me. Of course he knew I was there. With Willow at his side, he hadn't sensed me. Her pull was far too strong. Now that she closed the door between them, I knew his head cleared enough to feel the real threat.

Four. Seven. No. I sensed at least a dozen wolves headed straight for me. Shit. His pack was massive. Even some of the largest packs in upper Michigan and Canada weren't that big.

I wondered how many had joined him willingly. One move, one word, and he would order them to kill first and ask questions later. One on one, I liked my chances against Soren. He may be strong, powerful, a pack leader. But, he hadn't come of age under the harsh landscape of the Siberian wilderness like I had.

Thirteen. Fourteen including Soren himself. Strong as I was, I knew I couldn't take on that many wolves alone.

As much as it killed me, my best move was to retreat. Regroup.

I pulled back to the shadows and followed the trail along the hidden stream. I knew there was a lake out there somewhere. It wasn't ideal, but if I could get to it before they caught the full force of my scent, I could keep them away.

Payne.

I needed to call Payne and let him know what was going on here. I didn't care how much Soren paid him for this job,

Wolfguard wasn't in the business of helping wolf shifters on their way to becoming *Tyrannous Alpha*.

Somehow, I managed to come back into myself. I found the scattered remnants of my clothes and got dressed. My cellphone was still in my jacket pocket. I pulled it out and punched in Payne's number.

The call wouldn't go through. There was no cell service out here. Damn. It meant I'd have to get closer to the main house. Doing so put me at risk of detection from Soren's pack, but I had to chance it. There was no way I was leaving this place without Willow safely beside me. From the looks of things out at the gazebo, I knew she'd agree.

How in the hell had her family let it get so far with this guy? As much as I wanted to rip Jason Soren to pieces, I had fantasies about doing the same to Daniel Rousseau. To hell with how connected he was.

From the looks of it, Willow was nothing more than chattel to the both of them. Soren must have sensed what I did about Willow when she was just a kid. I nearly doubled over as I let that thought fully form in my mind.

Willow told me she first met Soren through her father when she was fourteen years old. God. It meant he'd tried to groom her. All these years. She said she'd confided things in him. She said he made her feel safe. It was only when she finally got out on her own and moved to Denver, she started to get out from her father and Jason Soren's influence. No wonder they'd fought so hard to keep her at home.

I realized with cold, stark, clarity, that's exactly why they hired me to bring her here. They knew she might try to run. Oh, God. I had helped them. I had talked her into coming here and telling Jason how she felt. I had played right into their fucking hands. I came to the edge of the woods on the north side of the house, away from the gazebo. I sensed Willow on the third floor. She was back in her suite of rooms. She was alone. For now.

I pulled up Payne's number again. The call immediately dropped. I was still getting a no service warning. It made no sense. I had seen a cell tower right off the main road leading up to the Soren estate. It couldn't be more than a mile away.

I turned off the phone, then powered it up again. Still nothing.

I had two choices. I could move to another part of the grounds and try again. Or, I could leave the property and head into town and call from there.

But...then I'd be leaving Willow here alone, unprotected.

Shit.

I felt Soren's pack. They had mostly dispersed after not finding their quarry in the woods. I knew it was more than that though. The minute Willow was away from Soren's direct sight and touch, he came back into himself. He was in control. As much as it tore at me, I knew Willow might very well be in more danger with me here watching her.

But, I couldn't leave without telling her what I planned. I made a promise to her. In another couple of hours, the sun would go down. I'd told her to meet me by the stables. With any luck, she'd find a way to get there.

So, I would wait. Willow may not have known exactly what Jason Soren was, but her instincts were good. I could sense those too. She knew he meant her harm. She knew he wasn't who she'd grown up believing he was. If she could keep her head, I could figure out a way to get her out of here without bringing the whole pack down on us.

It was a good plan. It might have even worked. But, as I receded back into the relative safety of the woods, with one wrong step everything went to hell.

He was pissing on a huge maple tree, his back to me. I'd been so focused on Willow, I hadn't heard him. A branch cracked beneath my foot as I took a step. He froze. Turning to the side, his wolf eyes flashed.

Just a beta wolf. A low-level lackey. His mind was thick and dumb. But, he had a voice. It only took the span of a heart-beat before he called to the pack.

"Son of a bitch," he said, then he shifted on a dime. His wolf was pale gray and skinny. His eyes sallow. I knew I could probably take him down with my bare hands without even shifting. But it wasn't just him.

They heard the call. The woods became ringed with yellow eyes as the rest of Soren's pack closed in. There were four to the left. Two to the right. The skinny gray wolf faced off with me. I made half a turn, planning to shoot for the small clearing over his left shoulder.

The three behind me struck at once, tearing the flesh from my back.

I let out a great howl and swiped my arm in a great arc. I was half in my wolf before my blow landed. I hit one wolf hard enough to knock him out before he hit the ground.

That was the last thing I remember before five more wolves leaped at me and the air went out of my lungs.

My ribs cracked. Blood poured from a gash at my temple. They drove me to my knees. I supposed I should have taken some small comfort in the fact that it took ten of them to bring me down.

There was a leader among them. Probably Soren's second in command. He was the only one of them not to shift. He stood over me as I doubled over. I tried to stand. I looked up at him, blood pouring into my eyes. He bared his teeth and curled his fists. It took six of them to hold me down as he landed a punishing blow to my jaw and all the lights went out.

CHAPTER TWELVE

WILLOW

I paced in front of my bedroom window. Jason had given me a suite of rooms in the east wing of the house. I had my every need attended to. A staff waiting on me hand and foot down to every detail such as drawing my bath. But as each moment ticked by, I knew this was nothing more than my prison.

There was something out there, watching me. I could see the woods from the window, dark, expansive. I waited until the moon rose high.

There was one mercy. Jason had left for the day and instructed his staff to let me take my meals in my room if that's what I wanted. I became keenly aware of the only thing I really did want above all else.

Val.

I should have met him the night before, but I couldn't get away. There was always someone with me, checking in on me. They were kind, attentive, but I knew every well-meaning face from the housekeepers to the cook to Kenneth Ramsey were all my jailers.

On the afternoon of the third day at the Soren House, something made me venture out.

There had been no word from Val. My heart sank, knowing he had probably just done exactly what Jason asked him to. He had taken his payment and gone back to his job. Because, that's all I was to him, wasn't it?

"Can I get anything for you, Miss Rousseau?" Naomi, one of the house managers stood at the top of the staircase. She had a tablet in her hand and was busy giving instructions to a younger maid named Caddie who I'd just met this morning.

"I'm fine," I said. "I just need some fresh air. Mr. Soren showed me the path through the rose garden the other day. I think I'd like to go walk it again."

Naomi smiled. "It's a beautiful day. Enjoy it. Do you want me to have your dinner brought to your rooms again?"

"Is it okay if I let you know when I get back?"

"Of course." She turned back to Caddie.

My heart raced as I made my way down the stairs. I wondered what would happen if I went through the rose garden and right on down into the woods. Part of me wanted to try, just to see.

I had every intention of heading through the French doors off the dining room. My heart raced with the prospect of even that much freedom. As much as I wanted to see Val again, I wanted my father too. I had zero contact with him since I left Denver. That was more than strange. Jason told me he had called in to check up on me but never asked to speak to me in person. But, he would be here in just a few days' time. Daniel Rousseau would be the man of the hour at my very own engagement party. My stomach churned just thinking about it.

I never made it to the dining room or the French doors or the rose garden. Instead, voices compelled me. There was no one in the grand foyer. Naomi and the housekeeping staff were still making their way through the east wing. The cooks were busy preparing dinner. Not even Ramsey popped his head out as he usually did when I left my rooms.

The voices were coming from the study. My pulse quickened as I recognized them. One was Jason. So, the staff had lied. He wasn't away on business again. That was the bad news. The good news was, he hadn't yet come to see me.

"He hasn't said a word." I didn't recognize the voice. I got bold and stepped closer to the doorway to the study. There was a tiny alcove and sitting area right next to the study. It was the perfect reading spot, overlooking the garden. Beside it was another door leading outside. On a whim, I opened it. I winced, waiting for some silent alarm to go off, alerting Jason or the rest of his staff that I'd gotten loose.

Nothing happened.

I stepped outside. An overhang kept me in shadows as I edged closer to the window to the study. The voices were still loud and clear. Only now, I could steal a glance at the faces they belonged to.

Jason sat behind his desk. Ramsey stood at his shoulder. Two other men stood in front of the desk as though Jason hadn't given them permission to sit.

They were tall, like Jason. Like Val. In fact, as I stood and watched them, I noticed a familiar quality about all of them. They each had an intensity to their eyes that made them glint. Corded muscles and broad frames made them look almost like a different species from Kenneth Ramsey with his long, wiry build. But, Jason looked different somehow. I hadn't noticed it before, but, he seemed bigger, more muscular. I wondered if he'd taken steroids in the last few years.

"I think the steel might be affecting him more than we expected." One of the men standing in front of Jason's desk spoke. He and the other man had the same ruddy complexions, closely cropped beards and black as midnight hair. They could be brothers.

"Maybe," Jason said. "And I don't know whether that's good or bad. As long as it's keeping him quiet, it'll do for now."

"I just don't understand it," Ramsey chimed in. "If he's a problem, you know I'll handle it."

Jason let out a sigh. He folded his hands at his desk. His ring flashed and he picked up an odd-looking keychain. It was gold, rimmed with diamonds. There was just one key on it. He spun it on his index finger.

"I don't pay you to understand, Kenneth."

"Mr. Soren," one of the black-haired muscleheads said, "We really could have handled this job. If you didn't want me or Rawley near Willow, I understand. But, Wolfguard?"

My heart twisted. Me. They were talking about me. And Wolfguard? That was Val's security firm.

"You do what I tell you," Jason said. He narrowed his eyes. When he did, both men before him squeezed their faces tight as if they were in pain. I watched as Jason exhaled. At the same time, the men relaxed.

What the actual hell was going on?

"It's not for us to question the ways of the ring," Ramsey said.

Jason shot him a look. I couldn't see his exact expression from here, but it was enough to make Ramsey blanch. Then, Jason turned back to his two associates.

"This wasn't an indictment of either of you or your work for me. In fact, I know full well if Willow had been in your care, she never would have tried to run again. But, there's more going on than just Willow. She's here. She's safe. Rousseau will be here in a few days. I just need you to keep doing what you do. I can't afford to have any more mistakes. You keep our guest under control. He's just as important as she is. If he wakes up, you tell me."

Jason kept twirling the gold key ring on his index finger. The diamonds flashed, casting a prism on the wall. It was hypnotic.

I shuddered thinking what would have happened if these two men got their wish and they'd shown up to get me from my apartment instead of Val.

But where the hell was he now? And what did Jason mean with these cryptic references to Wolfguard? *He's just as important as she is.* Did he mean Val?

My head started to spin in time with Jason's keyring. The hairs pricked on the back of my neck and I moved away from the window.

I found myself edging backward toward the rose garden. It's where I was supposed to be, after all. I didn't know whether Jason had anyone following me without my knowing about it. I felt alone. I felt hopeless.

This whole thing was insane. I'd be forced to marry a man I now feared to keep my father out of prison or worse. And if I went through with it all, what then?

An image flashed of the last time Jason kissed me. He had been cruel, demanding. I could *feel* the lust coursing through him, primal and wild. Possessive. Every cell in my body rejected it. He was different. Or I was. Either way, I felt like I could kill him before I let him touch me like that.

My skin burned for something else. Something just as primal. Desire thundered through me, taking my breath away. I hadn't expected it. It came unbidden.

Before I knew what was happening, I broke into a run. The woods called to me even as I knew they represented something dangerous. I couldn't see them. I didn't know where they were, but I felt certain down to the bone that Jason had either guards posted along the property or an alarm system that would call me out.

I didn't know where I was going. I just knew I couldn't go back to the house. Not yet. Not until...

I found myself at the stables. I wasn't even sure how I got here. I hadn't been back here since I was fourteen or fifteen years old. The place looked exactly the same. Newly painted with bright red, the barn loomed before me. Two of Jason's horses whinnied near the electrical fence. I went to the chestnut thoroughbred and ran my hand down his face. He calmed instantly. I had half a mind to mount him bareback and jump the damn fence.

Instead, I ducked beneath it, heading straight for the barn. It would be quiet in there. I knew a tucked away place high in the loft. Maybe I could just hide out for an hour or so and think.

Two more horses brayed in their stalls as I stepped inside. I felt a wave of heat. It hit me square in the chest, making my heart stop for a moment.

There was movement in the shadows. I felt pulled like a tractor beam. I made my way down to the very last stall.

What I saw there sucked the air from me. My legs gave out. I gripped the side of the stall door to keep from falling.

"Val," I whispered. "My God!"

He was badly hurt, laying on his side. His breath came in ragged pants. He was naked from the waist up. His suit pants were tattered. His shoes missing. But, it was his back that shocked me the most.

He had deep gashes marring his muscled torso and back. It looked like he'd been mauled by something big. The back of his neck was nearly torn away.

I collected myself and stepped quietly into the stall. By the light of the rising moon, I saw the chains around his wrist. They were wound around his forearms and crossed through a heavy loop bolted to the floor.

"Val," I whispered. I reached for him, my fingers trembling.

I gently touched his shoulder on the only patch of skin I could find not torn open.

He jerked backward, as if my touch sent an electric shock through him. It had a similar effect on me. When he opened his eyes, something was wrong with them. They blazed almost neon blue. It didn't make sense here in the shadows. The light played tricks on my vision. I swore his teeth looked like fangs.

"Val," I said again, finding my own strength. "God. What did they do to you?"

He came into himself. Val jerked up to a sitting position and shuffled back against the wall. He had angry welts beneath his eyes. He'd been badly beaten. Tortured.

"Who did this to you?" I asked, but I already knew the answer.

"Willow," he said, his voice scratched and raw. "You have to leave. Don't let them find you here."

"Jason," I said. "He hurt you. Val, you need a doctor."

He gave me a sad smile and lifted his arms. The chains made a heavy rattle.

I bolted to my feet and felt along the wall. I scanned the equipment bench and tack on the far wall looking for a...

It hit me like a thunderbolt.

The key. The prism of light it made as Jason twirled the ring around his finger.

"I know where the key is," I said. "At least...I think I do. I'll figure this out. I'll get you out of here."

I went to him, sliding to my knees. Val winced as I placed a hand to his jaw. His skin burned hot. It ignited something in me as well.

"I'm so sorry," I said. I didn't understand everything that was happening. But, I knew in my heart what had happened to Val was because of me.

"He's going to kill you, isn't he?" I said.

Val gritted his teeth. "He's going to try. But, Willow, I don't care about that. I can take care of myself. Despite...what this looks like. You have to get the hell out of here. If you keep to the north of the property. Head through the woods. Follow the stream. Keep running and don't look back. But, go now. They'll be back. Does Soren even know you left the house?"

"He...I told the housekeeper I wanted to take a walk through the garden. Nobody stopped me. Jason is...I saw him from the window. He's in his study. Two other men. Big ones. And Kenneth Ramsey."

"Then go now," he said. "He'll track you here. I can buy you some time."

"Track me?" I asked.

"Willow, go! You might not get another chance. But you cannot be here when Jason figures out you're gone."

He was right. I knew it in my heart. I also knew this might be the only chance I'd have to make a run for it and take charge of my own fate.

Fate.

I don't know why, but the word echoed through my mind with the force of a thunderclap.

My eyes were drawn to those heavy chains on Val's wrists. He was strong. But no man could be strong enough to break them.

"No," I said. "I have another plan. I'm not leaving you here like this. I'm going to figure out a way to get you out. Trust me."

Val's eyes widened. In the distance, I heard a wolf howl. But, that was impossible. My ears were now playing tricks on me along with my eyes.

He shouted in a whisper, trying to call me back. But, I was already gone, running at top speed back toward the house.

CHAPTER THIRTEEN

VAL

Had I dreamt it? Sweat poured from me. My vision blurred. It felt like I had an anvil sitting on my chest. Willow's scent lingered. Her desire. Her fear.

I rolled to my side and pain gripped me.

This was no dream. My arms were on fire. My wrists. Something had taken a bite out of me. The back of my neck ached.

Soren's pack. Thirteen on one they'd dragged me here and chained me to this wall. I pulled at the cuffs. It was no use. Dragonsteel. Soren had used iron forged with Dragonfire. It was the only metal strong enough to keep a shifter like me in chains.

How he'd gotten ahold of the stuff was probably a bigger problem than just my predicament.

"I think I know where he keeps the key."

"Willow!" I whispered into the darkness. She can't have been serious. God. No matter what else happened, she had to stay away. If Soren found her trying to help me...

A growl ripped from me. I yanked the chains. I would tear the fucking barn down and drag it with me if I had to. I would not let him touch her. I would go through all thirteen or more of Jason Soren's pack if that's what it took.

It was no use. The man knew what he was doing when he built this place. The chains were secured by a metal loop bolted the floor. It was anchored by another block of metal buried deep in the ground. That was made of dragonsteel too.

New horror sunk in. The barn was built around the chains and the structure had to be at least a hundred years old. What in the hell was Soren's family into?

Payne had to know. I had to figure out a way to get loose and get word to him. I was starting to believe the shoddy cellphone reception was no accident either.

I closed my eyes and tried to call forth my wolf. I knew it was useless to try, but I needed it. I felt the beast clamoring to get out. He clawed from the inside.

Then...nothing. My wolf's heart went quiet. The dragon-steel did more than just keep me chained to the floor. Its ancient magic kept my own from rising.

The morning sun peeked through the slats in the roof. I tried to make myself still. I tried to listen for Willow.

Her touch still lingered on my chest. I craved her. She was out there. Deep in my soul, I could sense her heart beating.

Mine. She was mine. I would kill or die for her if it came to it.

The barn door creaked open. Two gray wolves came in, their tails low. They took sentry on either side of the stall, their teeth bared. I sensed four other wolves surrounding the perimeter of the barn. I knew the rest stayed hidden in the woods, ready to give chase if I managed to get past those closest. I longed for the chance to try.

Then, the air seemed to grow thick and cold. Jason Soren walked in. His yellow wolf eyes glinted, but he kept his beast in check.

He came to the stall opening. His wolves snapped their teeth. I pulled at the chains, envisioning wrapping them around his damn neck and squeezing until his eyes bulged.

"You're awake," he said. "Good. I'll have them bring you something to eat."

"Fuck you," I spat.

Soren was dressed more casually then I'd seen him. He was barefoot, in jeans and a faded t-shirt. So, he wanted to be ready to shift. I couldn't help but curl my lips into a smile. Even with over a dozen members of his pack and the dragonsteel binding me, the asshole was still a little afraid of what I might do.

"You want to kill me," he said, his tone calm. It was more an observation than an accusation.

I had just enough beast simmering that I answered with a snap of my teeth. Soren's wolves responded, lunging forward. He put a hand up. In an instant, they fell back, tails tucked flat between their legs.

"It's good that you want to kill me," he said. "How would you do it? With your bare hands? Would you try to squeeze the life out of me? Or would you rather let your wolf out?"

I growled. He edged closer. It seemed he knew exactly how far the chains would stretch.

"Right," he said, smiling. "It'd be your wolf then. I suppose that's how I'd do it too. Have you ever killed a man in your wolf? Or another wolf? You feel their lifeblood flowing. There's a taste. It changes after they've crossed the brink and they know they're going to die. It sweetens. Some say it's better than sex. I don't know if I agree. I suppose it depends on the partner. Now...Willow...I think her nectar will be the sweetest thing I've ever tasted."

My vision went pure red. Fire shot through my veins as I strained against the chains. My heart thundered in my head. Blood. Pain. Death. My wolf took over, even though he couldn't get out.

It was madness. Chaos. This bridge between beast and man.

Bloodlust.

Jason Soren stood at the center of it. His voice filled my head.

"Let go," he said. "Submit."

My growl tore through me. I felt his pack. Their thoughts joined as one. They were calm. Soren was in control.

"Submit!"

Blood poured down my arms where I tried to throw off the chains. My blood. My strength. I was an Alpha. Without his pack, I knew I was far stronger than Jason Soren could ever be.

I pushed against him with my mind. I wasn't human. I wasn't wolf. I was something in between.

The force of it knocked Soren back against the wall. He bared his teeth. His wolves charged. They were inches from my face.

At the last second, Soren got control and called them back. I was close enough to hear the deafening siren of his command. His wolves dropped, twitching on the ground with a keening howl.

Then, Soren rose and towered over me.

"You're strong," he said. "That'll make this all the better."

Did he really not know? "You're not too bright, are you?" I said. I knew I should keep my mouth shut. The more I talked, the more power I gave him.

I dared him to come closer. Just an inch. I could crush his windpipe in the span of a heartbeat. If I could just get to him before he had a chance to send a command to the pack.

"You know," he said. "I never believed in fate. I mean, I know we were all raised on it. Fated mates. An Alpha's one true love. I've never seen it. Never felt that. I think it's just another fairytale we get told. My parents weren't fated. It was an arranged marriage. My mother was the daughter of a powerful Alpha from the Yukon. My father descended from the Alphas who led the strongest packs of Virginia since before it was a colony. I have Monacan blood flowing through me. My parents? They were happy though."

I turned from him. Though I'd broken his weak attempt at trying to subjugate me into his pack, the effort of it drained me. Between that and the dragonsteel's magic, I felt a blackout coming on.

"You believe it though, don't you?" Soren said. He edged just a hair's breadth closer.

I wouldn't look at him.

"Or...maybe you *didn't* believe it until...she crossed your path."

I must have flinched. Soren's smile widened.

"Willow," he said. "You know, I knew she was a wolf's mate

the second I saw her. It's in her blood. I did some digging into her genealogy. I couldn't find him though. Her shifter ancestor. I know some say wolves' mates have to have some dormant shifter blood in them somewhere. That if it weren't for a witch's curse a thousand years ago, they'd all be shifters too. I don't know. I suppose it doesn't much matter."

He leaned against the wall of the stall. "What *does* matter is that she was born to this. You felt it too. Admit it. She smells so, so sweet. I'll let you in on a little secret. She tastes even better."

His eyes flashed. My head spun with the image of Soren's hands on Willow in the gazebo. He'd kissed her.

"The sweetest nectar," he said. "It makes your blood sing. That's just her mouth. Imagine how good she'll taste down..."

I launched myself at him. Two floorboards cracked in half, but the anchor held.

Soren didn't even flinch. His eyes though, they flashed bright red for an instant.

"You think she's yours," he said. "I can feel it pouring off of you. I can almost hear it in your head. You're telling yourself she was made for you. That's good. You just keep telling yourself that. This time tomorrow night, I'll make her mine while you rot here in your dragon chains."

"She's not your mate," I said.

"She will be," he answered. "One bite at the base of her neck. You know how it goes. She'll start to crave me too. She'll be part of my pack. I'll hear her heartbeat alongside mine. Wherever she is...I'll always be able to find her. Just one bite. It'll be her coming out party."

He slapped my face. I stayed still as stone. He wanted my rage. He could use it against me. I had to keep my head. If I had a prayer of stopping him from marking Willow, I had to stay in control. I had to think.

"It'll be easier for you after that," he said.

God. Now I understood. He knew what Willow was to me. If he claimed her, it would make it that much easier the next time he tried to force me into his pack. He would use her as bait.

"I'll kill you," I said. "I don't care what you try to do to me. You won't be strong enough to stop me."

"I won't have to be," he smiled.

He gestured with his chin. The four wolves in the barn came to his side.

"Tomorrow night," Soren said. "You'll see the lights from the main house. In fact, maybe I'll move you there so you can hear better. I'm throwing a little engagement party. Plenty of important people will be there to see how beautiful my fiancée is. She'll be a star. And later, she'll be mine."

I had to force the vision of me ripping his throat out from

my head. He was right. My rage made it so much easier for him.

"Why?" I asked, not expecting him to respond.

"Because I need her," he said, surprising me. "For her family. For mine. And it turns out, this *is* fate at work. It's completely changed my way of thinking. Exciting, isn't it?"

I didn't get a chance to answer. One more flick of Soren's wrist and his wolves closed in.

Two clawed my chest. One drove me back against the wall. The dragonsteel held, but I landed a blow across his snout, sending him reeling end over end to the other side of the stall.

The fourth one shifted. He curled his fist and punched me. Pain exploded across my face as my nose broke. The blackness took over as I sank to the ground.

CHAPTER FOURTEEN

WILLOW

The dress was Valentino. Red. Strapless. Backless with a hard bodice that hugged me close, nearly constricting my breath. In that, it matched the theme of the night. I felt trapped in it.

My engagement gift hung just above my cleavage. It was a teardrop, ten-carat diamond. It matched my earrings.

The stylists had just left. My hair was pulled neatly into a French knot. My makeup was pristine. I hated myself this way. I slipped my feet into the four-inch, torturous heels that completed the look.

The guests had already begun to arrive. The show was about to begin. I left the mirror and went to the window. No light came from the barn. I could barely see it in the shadows.

But, I felt him. Val. If I closed my eyes and held my breath, I swear I could almost hear his heartbeat. It made no sense. Maybe the stress of the day was getting to me. But, early this morning, I could swear I felt his pain. For two days, I'd tried to find a way to get into Jason's study. God. It was crazy. I didn't even know for sure if the keyring he flashed was the one that would unlock Val's bindings. Except, something in my heart told me I was right. So, tonight might be my last chance to do something for him. It would be dangerous. But, with all the guests, Jason would be the most distracted.

There was a soft knock on the door. I jumped.

"Willow?"

My father's voice put a lump in my throat. He wasn't supposed to be here until later.

I ran to the door and flung it open. Tears threatened to fall, but I held them back.

"Daddy," I gasped.

He took my hands. His eyes glistened with tears he was trying to hold back too.

"Look at you," he said. "You look like...your mother." That same sadness deepened the lines in his face. For as much as he cared about Lisette, I knew my mother had been the love of his life. There were those who told me he'd never been the same since her accident. I was too young to remember a difference. But, I saw his pain clearly now.

He pulled me into a bone-crushing hug. He felt good. Strong. At the same time, part of me wanted to pull away and rail at him. If it weren't for him, I wouldn't be in this predicament. Jason Soren would have no hold on me. On either of us.

"I'm glad you're here," I said.

"What's wrong?" he asked.

I blinked fast, trying to keep those same tears at bay.

"Nothing. I'm just nervous. You know I don't like crowds. I don't like being the center of attention. And this...it's just not me." I gestured to the dress.

My father's smile tightened. "It'll be good for the family," he said. "Jason cares for you. He'll make you happy."

"I don't love him," I blurted out.

My father's face fell. He took a step sideways and closed the door behind him.

"Then what the hell are we doing here?"

His words were a gut-punch.

"What?"

"Willow, do you think I'd force you to marry a man you don't care for?"

I flapped my arms to my sides. "Um...yes. You keep saying how good this will be for the family. I know what that means."

He put a hand to his stomach. "No. Do you hear me? No. But, cold feet are normal, Willow. And you and Jason...you haven't spent that much time together. This is all...it's a lot. This party wasn't my idea. It's Jason who wants to show you off. Maybe I should have been a little more forceful in trying to talk him out of it. He insisted it's what you both wanted."

No. I wanted to shout it. Nothing about this was what I wanted. I said nothing. Lisette and Jason's warnings echoed through my mind. I knew it was distinctly possible my own father didn't even realize the kind of trouble he was in.

"Willow," he said, taking me by the hands. "If you need more time...if you're not ready for this..."

"It's too late," I whispered.

He leaned in, kissing the top of my head. "That's my girl. You really are so beautiful. Jason's the luckiest man in the world. Next to me, of course."

"Daddy," I said. "Can I ask you to do something for me?"

"I'll give you the world. You know that"

"I've never needed the world. It's just...Can you give me your trust?"

"You don't even have to ask."

"Right," I said. "But...like you said. This is all so over-whelming. I just think...At a certain point tonight, I might need to just get some air. Jason is...well...he's overprotective. And this place is crawling with security. We're all perfectly safe. It can be smothering though. So, if I give you a signal, can you make sure to cover for me? Like I said, just so I can take a minute to myself. Then I swear I'll be all right. I'll be everything you all want me to be."

My father smiled. "You want me to handle Jason if you need to slip away for a second?"

"Yes. Can you?"

"Of course. You know I'll always have your back."

I hugged him again and wished to God that was true. "And you know I always have yours. Even if we don't agree on everything."

There was another knock at the door. Naomi popped her head in.

"I'm sorry to disturb you. Mr. Soren asked that you both come down if you're ready. The main guests are here. He'd like to present you now."

Present me. Just like some trophy. I resisted the urge to say it. My father gave me his arm. He'd said all the right words to me tonight, but I couldn't help resenting his complicity. I was his prize too.

But, I felt relief flowing through me now that I'd formed the basics of a plan. When the time seemed right, I would slip away to the study and find that key. I just prayed it was still there.

As we walked to the top of the winding staircase into the main foyer, my heart didn't feel like my own. There was an undercurrent to my pulse. It was crazy. Impossible. And yet, I knew it was Val I sensed. He was out there. He was hurt. He was running out of time. We both were.

―――――

"There she is!" Jason's voice boomed. He stood at the bottom of the staircase wearing a crisp tuxedo. He looked every bit the dashing prince every girl dreamed about. For me, he'd become my nightmare. His gaze was predatory. His eyes glinted with that mysterious glow I thought only I could see.

On my father's arm, I descended the stairs. I kept my back straight. My smile tightly in place. Then, Jason took my hand. His skin burned through mine.

We made our way through a line of congratulations. Jason hadn't been kidding when he told me how important this night was for him...and for my father.

I recognized two U.S. senators, one, a presidential hopeful. Jason introduced me to no fewer than three federal judges. The implication was clear. These men and women had power and influence. The next time my father or one of his associates ended up on the wrong side of a RICO investigation, Jason had the pull to make it go away. And he had the pull to make it worse...much worse.

"Aren't you just the most delicious thing!" A chill ran down my spine as the wife of one of the federal judges put a hand on my arm. "Jason did not exaggerate your beauty, honey. I hope you know how lucky you are to have snagged this gorgeous hunk right here. I was trying to save him for one of my own girls."

"Oh, I'm aware of how lucky I am," I said, trying not to grit my teeth. Jason was charming. He found a way to shake hands with everyone here. My feet ached from standing in those impossible shoes. This role was more suited to someone like Lisette. She thrived on the elbow rubbing and always seemed to know exactly what to say.

The minutes ticked by, turning into hours. Jason's staff kept the drinks flowing. Liveried waiters attended to the needs of every guest. At nine, Jason moved the party into the grand ballroom where a live band played. Then, he asked me to dance.

The crowd parted and he led me to the center of the floor. A massive, glittering chandelier hung high in the domed ceiling. As the band struck up a tango, Jason led me around the floor.

There were oohs and ahs as he dipped and spun me. Somehow, I managed to keep up in my heels. Years ago, my father had made me take dance lessons. I was grateful for them now. I knew how important it was to him and to Jason for me to pull this off. If I could just bide my time. As we worked our way through the crowd, several of his guests asked Jason for a moment alone with him. I could only guess what favors they hoped he would grant.

As the music crescendoed and Jason twirled me one last time, I knew my moment was about to come. The glad-handing would take a break as the guests took to the dance floor.

Jason pulled me close. His lips brushed my ear sending a shiver through me. Once upon a time, it would have sent my blood humming with desire. There was a strange echo of that now. Despite everything else he was, Jason Soren was a compelling man. But now, I just wanted to get away.

"Come with me," he whispered. He took my hand as the crowd applauded. He led me through it with the same grace as the tango. We went down the corridor and he pushed through the door to the study.

My heart raced. All night. All week I had tried to find a way to steal away to this room. Jason walked right to the desk and sat on the edge. He pulled me to him so I was standing almost between his legs.

"You're amazing," he said. His eyes held an intoxicated glaze, but I'd never seen him take so much as a drop.

"Thank you," I said. "But, we should get back. My father's going to wonder where I am."

"He'll know you're with me," he said. Jason lifted a hand and cupped the back of my neck. His fingers played along my hairline. They burned. My breath caught.

"I want you," he said.

"Jason. Not here. Not now. We've waited this long. I know

it sounds old-fashioned, but at this point I want to wait until we get married."

He smiled. "I don't just want to fuck you, Willow. I said I *want* you. Here. Now. I can make you mine."

"I don't know what you're talking about."

"Yes. I think you do. I think you've known it all along. It's in you, Willow. And you don't even fully realize it."

I pulled away from him. My breath came in quick pants. It was stifling in here. I wanted to open a window. I wanted to run.

"I really think we should head back. You've got to meet in private with at least a dozen people before the night is over. I heard you promise them. There will be time enough for this...later."

Though, I had no idea what *this* meant. Still, my heart raced. Adrenaline coursed through me. I felt danger coming from him on a primal level. Staying here with him alone was bad.

He caught my arm and pulled me back.

"Let me go," I challenged him.

He cupped my neck again. Heat flamed at the base of my skull. I felt the strangest urge. A hunger I couldn't name. At the same time, those danger warning bells flared through me.

Something was seriously wrong. Sweat broke out on my brow.

"It won't hurt," he said. "In fact, it'll feel so good once I start. Let me taste you, Willow. You have no idea the kind of power it will bring."

He didn't say what he meant. Not the words. And yet, the truth of his desire hit me. I knew what he wanted. Good God. He meant to bite me where the heat flared hottest at the base of my neck.

"Jason...let's not..."

He moved so fast. He turned me, placing his hands on my neck. He had me against the desk, bending me at the waist. He ran his hand down my bare back then up my arms. He threaded his fingers through mine, pinning my palms to the desktop.

I felt his breath at my back. He licked a trail up my spine.

"You want my mark," he said. "I can feel it burning through you."

I pushed back. Jason was like a stone wall. Immovable. Powerful. Dangerous.

He licked the base of my skull. I didn't want this. It was as if my very blood recoiled at his touch. And yet, he was right about one thing. I did feel something. A need so powerful it took my breath away. But, Jason Soren was the wrong man.

"Let me go," I whispered. He inched forward. I felt his teeth scrape my flesh.

"No!"

A groan of pleasure escaped from him. A switch flipped inside of him. It was as if he were no longer human but fueled by some animal instinct I couldn't name.

Then, I knew. He didn't see me. Didn't hear me.

I slipped my right hand out of his and slid it across the surface of the desk. Jason didn't react. He just licked my neck again and positively purred.

The desk drawer was open slightly. I could feel the outline of his key ring with my fingers.

"Say you want it," he whispered. "I'll take it either way. I know what's good for you."

I closed my fingers around the keys. I could make a weapon out of them if I had to. I could drive them into Jason's temple if I reached back far enough.

"Jason!"

He let out a short growl then let me go.

I palmed the keys and straightened. As I turned, I caught a glimpse of Jason that froze my heart. I had to be seeing things. It was fear or adrenaline or something else I couldn't name. His eyes blazed nearly gold, the pupils were round and black. He bared his teeth but I saw fangs instead. His nose had changed, growing longer. He looked just like...

A wolf.

Then, in a flash, he was Jason again. My father stood at the doorway, his cheeks flushed.

Jason straightened his jacket and smoothed his hair.

"Daniel," he said.

"You need to get back to your guests," my father said. His eyes were locked on mine. I gave him a tiny nod.

"Of course," Jason said. "Willow?"

"If you don't mind," I said. "I'm going to hang back for a second. I need some air."

Jason looked from me to my father. I could see his thoughts as if they went across his forehead like a news crawl. Did he dare make a scene? Exert his power over my father?

Jason gave me a forced smile. "Just a few minutes, my love," he said.

"Don't worry," my father said. "I'll stay with her."

Jason worked something out for himself. He wasn't pleased, but he'd clearly decided not to push things further for now.

He shook my father's hands and made his way back to the party. As soon as we were alone, I felt like I might throw up.

"You okay?" my father asked.

I leaned in and kissed him. "I will be, Daddy. I will be. Do you think you can handle Jason for a few minutes? I really do need some air."

His lips were tight when he smiled. "Just a few," he said. "I don't like the idea of you roaming around alone out there."

"I can take care of myself," I said. I kissed my father one more time and let myself out the double doors.

There was no one out here. All of Jason's staff were inside attending to his guests. I hiked up my dress and ran as fast as my heels would take me.

CHAPTER FIFTEEN

VAL

I was out of my mind. Willow's heartbeat drummed in my head. She was scared. Panicked. Soren's scent was everywhere.

I pulled at the dragonsteel chains. It did nothing more than deepen the gauge in my wrists, but I didn't care. I was two seconds from chewing my damn arm off to get to Willow.

And then...she was there.

She was an angel. A vision in red and diamonds. She held the ends of her dress in one hand, and a keyring in the other.

"Val!" she gasped. She looked behind her. I scrambled to my feet.

She came to the entrance of the stall. Her breath heaved.

The heart-shaped bodice of her dress hugged her breasts, revealing tantalizing cleavage. She was Willow, but not. Her face, expertly painted to highlight her full, luscious red lips, the delicate arch of her brow. She looked like some red carpet-ready movie star.

Then, I saw the marks on her arm. Soren. He had grabbed her. Held her. His fingers digging into her skin hard enough to leave those marks. In a few hours, she would bruise.

I bared my teeth and tried to keep Willow from seeing. Predatory rage boiled through me. At the same time, so did desire.

I wanted her. All of her. Jason Soren couldn't make me submit, but he had driven me to the point of being almost feral.

"Val," Willow said again. She took a tentative step inside the stall. Her presence calmed me. I focused on steadying my breathing and straightened my back.

"How?" I managed.

She hesitated. She had no way of knowing what I was. But, she didn't have to. Her nature recognized mine, even if she couldn't connect it in the logical part of her brain yet. Soon enough, she would.

"Let me," she said, holding up the key ring. A single gold key dangled from the center of it. I didn't need to inspect it any closer to know it too was made of dragonsteel.

"How?" I asked again.

"I don't know," she said. "I don't know anything. It just...God. I'm probably losing my mind. The thing just sort of...called to me. And the way Jason was holding on to it, I just knew."

A growl vibrated through me. "He hurt you."

She smoothed a stray hair. I'd never seen her wear it up like that. It showed off the elegant curve of her shoulder and slope of her long neck.

I curled my fists at my sides. Her neck. I craved it. If she turned and exposed it to me, I wasn't sure even the dragon-steel would be enough to keep me from shifting.

She came to me, curious, but unafraid.

"Where is he?" I whispered.

"Up at the house. At the party. My father's covering for me, but I don't know how long he can. Give me your wrists."

I froze. I wanted nothing more than to be free of those chains. And yet, I wondered whether I could contain my wolf anymore without them.

Willow acted for me. She reached for me, pulling my arms toward her. Her touch sent fire through my veins. I saw her sharp intake of air, but she didn't let go.

Her fingers trembled as she worked the key into the lock. I held my breath.

The chains opened and fell to the floor with a thunderous rattle.

A moment. A heartbeat. Time stood still as Willow's eyes met mine.

Hear pulse skipped, but it wasn't fear I sensed. It was desire.

She broke the spell and took a step back. She turned slightly, looking down. I glimpsed the back of her neck and saw white for an instant.

I don't know what power allowed me to keep my wolf quiet. He stirred. He raged. But I didn't shift.

Willow had two tiny marks at the base of her neck. Soren had scraped her with his teeth. He meant to mark her.

I would kill him.

"Willow," I said, my voice dropping so low it barely sounding like my own.

I reached for her, gently taking her by the wrist. I turned her away from me so I could see her neck more fully.

There could be no doubt. These marks were fresh. She had no idea how close she had come to danger I couldn't protect her from.

"I have to get you away from here," I said. "Now."

Little by little, the rest of the world began to rush back in. I heard laughter. Clinking glass. Music. Soren's party continued. I sensed him in the center of a crowd of people. His pack dispersed, taking up positions where they could be ready for whatever their Alpha commanded.

"He's distracted," I said. "But, he won't stay that way for long. Jason Soren wants to hurt you. He wants to do things to you that..."

"I know," she said, slipping out of my grasp and facing me. She brought her hand up and covered the back of her neck with it.

"He was...Val, he was different. There's something wrong with him. He's changed from who he thought I was. Or...he was pretending with me the whole time. I'm afraid of him."

"You should be," I said.

"What do we do?"

"We leave. We run. Right now."

She looked back toward the house. I couldn't read her mind. She wasn't mine yet. Not fully. Maybe not ever. I would *never* claim this woman if she didn't want it, no matter how badly the urge burned through me. But I could feel Willow's mood shifting. She seemed to understand what I was telling her on a primal level.

"He's not going to give me up without a fight," she said.

"Probably not," I answered. "But I can't protect you here. Not on his territory. There are too many of them."

She didn't ask me what I meant. She simply nodded.

"Willow," I said. "It has to be now. Soren's going to figure out you left the party. He's going to send his men back here to deal with me. We have to be long gone by then."

Her eyes widened. "My father," she said. "I have to warn him. I can't leave him alone with Jason."

I clenched my jaw. I didn't want it to come to it, but if I had to, I would throw Willow over my shoulder and get her out of here that way.

"Your father can take care of himself for now. Soren wouldn't be stupid enough to harm him in front of his guests."

"You don't understand," she said, frantic. "There is something *wrong* with him. He's not...Val...he's...I don't know if it's drugs. It's something. He's like a sociopath. I don't know what I ever saw in him."

I put my hands on her shoulders, holding her as gently as an egg. She was stronger than that though. I could feel it in the way she tensed her muscles and stiffened her spine. I could feel it in the way her soul called to mine. Touching her made me stronger too.

"Willow, your father is safer if you're far away from Jason Soren. If he knew how Soren wanted to hurt you, if he were standing here right now, he'd tell you to run. He'd tell you to get the hell away from this place and never look back. And, if he didn't...then your father doesn't have your best interests at heart. I do."

She blinked.

"Willow, your father has been pushing you to marry that man since you were fourteen years old. I have no idea if he truly understands what kind of man he is. For his sake, I hope he doesn't. But, you have to look out for yourself first. And you have to let me help you. I might be the only one who can."

"He knows," she said. "I think he knows. Right before I left him in the study, my father told me I didn't have to marry Jason if I didn't want to."

"Good enough," I said. "Then there is no doubt in my mind he would want this for you. But, we're running out of time."

"He'll kill him," Willow said. Her first tear fell and it gutted me. "I know it in my heart. If Jason doesn't get what he wants, he'll go after my dad."

"Listen to me," I said. "Jason Soren isn't the only one with powerful allies. My brother is Andre Kalenkov. That name may not mean anything to you, but it does to Jason. And the men I work for, the men he hired to bring you here...God...I swear to you, I didn't know when I took this assignment. I never would have led you here if I did. I swear that on my life. But, when I tell Payne Fallon what's really going on, Soren will have Wolfguard to contend with too. We'll come back for your father. We can protect him."

My heart thundered as a plaintive howl cut through the air. Soren's attention was diverted with the party, but wouldn't be for long. If we had the whisper of a chance of getting off this property without the entire Soren pack down our throats, it had to be now.

"Trust me," I said, holding my hand out to Willow. My

heart beat a strong, steady pace. I felt hers beneath it, slowing to meet mine.

She licked her lips. I watched a tremor go through her. Her body was telling her the answer. I just prayed she would let her mind open to the truth.

She took one glance back at the house. "Swear it," she whispered.

"I swear it on my life. I will keep you safe from Soren and anyone else who tries to get to you. And I'll do everything in my power to make sure he doesn't come after your father."

She nodded. She took my hand. New strength flowed through me.

I wanted to throw her over my shoulder and run as fast as I could. It would scare her. She would never understand my speed. So, I did the next best thing.

I opened the next stall and led a magnificent, black stallion out. I cupped my hands and helped Willow climb on his back. There was no time for a saddle. Then, I leaped up in front of her. One swift kick to the horse's flanks and we were racing out of the barn toward the woods.

CHAPTER SIXTEEN

Val

Twin instincts propelled us, mine and the horse's. We headed north, through the woods, beyond the stream.

There were wolves at my back. I felt them. I heard them. They tried to catch my scent, but we were moving too fast and the horse helped.

Willow had a death grip around my waist. She shifted her weight as the horse drove on. She was no novice rider. I was grateful for that.

I gave the horse his head. We leaped over a small hill. Willow's hair came loose. The branches clawed at her, leaving strands of her long hair as beacons for Soren's pack as they tried to track her.

There was no help for it. There was only speed and

distance. With each pounding crunch of the horse's hooves, I felt my own power returning. I'd been in a fog of dragon magic for far too long. My wolf raged inside of me, but he was a part of me again. The horse felt it. He whinnied, but he recognized what I was and submitted to my command.

"There!" Willow shouted.

I saw it too.

We'd nearly arrived at the riverbed. It stretched long and wide. We had come to the place where the horse could no longer go.

He came to a halt, kicking up dirt. His legs reared up. Willow slid backward. I caught her with my arm and guided her gently down. I put a hand on the horse's neck, touching my forehead to his.

"Go," I whispered. "Stay along the river, my friend. Give them all a run for their money."

The horse stomped the ground. He focused one, great, black eye on Willow. She nuzzled his ear.

"Thank you," she said. "I wish I had a treat for him."

The horse snorted, then took off, running east right along the riverbank.

"That'll throw them for a while at least," I said.

"Throw who?" she asked. "Dogs? You think Jason will send dogs after us? I thought I heard…"

She either couldn't or wouldn't finish the thought.

"The bridge is that way." She pointed west.

"I know. But we can't afford to take it. We need to swim for it. The river is shallowest here. Keep a hand on my shoulder."

"We're swimming?" she asked. "Val..."

"I asked you to trust me," I said. "Yes. Jason will send dogs. They're already coming. The horse will buy us time. The river will throw them completely. But we need to go right now."

She looked down. I'd forgotten what she was wearing. The river would ruin her dress.

"Willow..."

She put a hand up. "It's only Valentino." Smiling, she pushed past me and dove into the river head first.

Smiling, a rush of adrenaline went through me as I dove in after.

Willow swam with the skill of an Olympian, her arms slicing through the water. She was strong. I was stronger. I caught up to her.

Midway across, Willow took my direction and put a hand on my shoulder. I whipped through the water. It was cold and exhilarating as I swam against the current.

We reached the other side.

Gasping, I pulled Willow out onto the sandy shore. Her hair slicked back. Water dripped from her nose.

She lost her shoes somewhere along the way and the dress clung to her like a second skin now. I tried to keep my gaze from traveling to the seductive shape of her hips and breasts.

"We made it," she said.

And we had.

This was somewhere near Bush Creek. We were at least a few miles outside the boundaries of Jason Soren's property. Now, I just needed to find a phone and call for backup from Wolfguard.

Something changed in Willow. She seemed freer. Happier. It was as if her body recognized the hold Jason Soren had tried to exert and now she was at least temporarily out of his reach.

I wanted to scoop her up and kiss her. I wanted to make her mine. But, as we picked our way through the brush and found a trail leading up to the nearby highway, another truth thundered through me with each heartbeat.

It had all been way too easy. I didn't yet know his game. But there was no doubt in my mind that Jason Soren had just let us go and the worst was yet to come.

CHAPTER SEVENTEEN

WILLOW

It's a strange thing how much we rely on plastic and technology. Val and I caught a ride with a trucker as soon as we climbed up to the highway.

It was a miracle the guy let us in his cab. I couldn't imagine what we must have looked like. Me in sopping wet Valentino. Val shirtless, scratched up, in ripped jeans and his...well...Val-ness. He looked positively feral. I supposed that's why the guy knew not to cross him.

He gave us a ride all the way past Richmond to some tiny little town I hadn't heard of. We could offer him nothing but an old-fashioned thank you. I didn't think to bring my backpack when I stole out to that barn. Val had been stripped of everything but the tattered pants he wore by Jason's men.

Val gave the trucker a two-fingered wave as he pulled out of the gas station. There was a motel beside it flashing a vacancy sign. To me it looked like heaven. It was just past dawn. I was starving, exhausted, and the adrenaline rush of the night's events was starting to wear off.

"Come on," Val said. He bent down and gestured for me to hop on his back. I was barefoot. So was he, but it didn't seem to bother him. Smiling, I climbed on.

Val walked us across the parking lot to the hotel.

There was a young kid behind the counter in the lobby.

"One room," Val said. The kid looked us up and down and set his jaw to the side. God knew what he thought. Probably that I was some kinky sex worker with the state of my dress.

"Wait here," Val whispered. He went to talk to the kid while I plopped into a deep, leather chair. I was so drowsy, I could barely keep my head up.

Val spoke in hushed whispers. He gave the kid a number. He dialed the phone and held it to his ear. Whoever he called, whatever they said, the kid's face grew serious and he just kept nodding and saying, "Yes, sir."

Two minutes later, Val walked away from the desk with a key card.

I shook my head and took his offered hand.

"Do I even want to know?" I asked.

"Probably not."

He led me back outside and down the exterior corridor. We took the corner room, 117.

Val swiped the key card and we stepped inside. It was sparse with one king bed. Clean. Heaven.

"I need a shower," I declared.

"Take your time," he said. "I've got a few more calls to make. The kid said there's a robe for you on the hook behind the door."

I raised a brow. "A robe? In a motel?"

Val gave me a sheepish smile. "Uh...yeah...I guess this is the honeymoon suite."

"Oh...uh...You're right. I don't think I even want to know."

Val went to the landline phone at the night table. I closed the bathroom door and peeled off my dress.

In the mirror, I could see the faint beginnings of bruising on my arm where Jason had grabbed me. The back of my neck still burned where his teeth grazed me. Something had happened. I put a hand on my neck. It hurt when he did it. But, ever since then...ever since I took Val's hand...I had a new sensation there. A different kind of burn.

A craving.

I closed my eyes and imagined what it would feel like if Val bit me there. My eyes snapped open. I was losing it. I was exhausted.

I slipped into the shower and turned the jet on full blast, not even caring that the water came out ice cold.

When I finished, I heard Val hang up. His tone was grave. He was angry. I put the robe on. White, plush terrycloth. Its duplicate hung on a second hook on the back of the door.

I felt a little vulnerable as I stepped out of the bathroom. I wore nothing but the robe and the air hit my sensitive parts.

"Any luck?" I asked.

Val ran a hand across his jaw. "More or less. We need to sit tight. I'll scare up some breakfast for you."

I sank to the edge of the bed, feeling exhausted again.

"You should get some sleep," he said.

"What about you? Val, you've been through far worse than I have."

The moment I said it, something clicked in place. A cognitive dissonance made my brain buzz.

Val had been tortured. I'd seen the wounds all over him. Deep gashes on his back. Claw marks on his face. His eyes had nearly been swollen shut two days ago.

Now, as he stood here before me, there wasn't a mark on him. His perfect, chiseled muscles still glistened with a sheen of sweat, but every single scratch on him had already healed except for the one high up on his left shoulder near the base of his neck.

My heart raced. I slowly rose. Val gave me a quizzical look. Then, his face hardened. He knew. He knew I knew.

As if pulled by a tractor beam, I went to him. My fingers trembling, I reached up and touched his face. His perfect face. Nothing marred it. There was only a scruffy, three-day-old beard.

"Val," I whispered.

Other things clicked into place. Questions I never asked.

He'd run with such tremendous speed as we climbed up the hill to the highway. He found me on the train as if he'd tracked my scent.

My pulse raced. Instinct drove me. I placed a flat hand on his chest. I felt Val's heart beating slow, strong, steady. The pace of it matched my own. When my pulse tripped, so did his. Matched. Joined.

Another word whispered its way through my thoughts.

Mine.

His.

Fate.

I jerked my hand away.

"Val," I said.

I saw the tension in his shoulders ease. It was as if he had just geared up to tell me some lie, then let go. There was nothing between us now but the truth.

I knew it.

I'd always known it.

I thought something was wrong with Jason. There wasn't. There had been something wrong with me. I had kept myself blind to it until now.

I don't know what made do it. Instinct. Exhaustion. Maybe I was crazy.

I went to Val, rising up on my tiptoes. I took his face between my palms. I pulled him down to me.

A groan escaped his lips. He put his hands on my elbows, but he didn't pull away from me.

"The truth," I whispered. "I need to know the truth."

"There's nothing I can say..."

He was right. There were no words.

"Show me!" I shouted.

"Willow."

Instinct took over. Passion. I kissed him. His lips were soft at first, then grew demanding.

My blood sang. My body ached with pleasure. With the truth. I'd demanded it. I railed against it.

He was healed. He shouldn't be healed.

My mind flashed to the first night at Jason's as I looked out my bedroom window. Twin eyes flashed in the dark. Watching over me. Ready to kill or die for me.

A wolf. I had seen a wolf.

When we left Jason's I heard them too.

Truth. Fate. It was all too impossible.

Before I knew what was happening, I bit down hard, catching Val's bottom lip between my teeth.

I tasted his blood and my heart exploded.

Desire nearly knocked my feet out from under me. But, Val held me up. I couldn't breathe.

I craved.

Finally, I tore myself away. Gasping, I stumbled to the other side of the room.

I heard Val pant. The air swirled with magic. Val held his head in his hands. He couldn't control it any more than I could.

I blinked hard, trying to understand. Then, I knew there had never been any mystery at all. I had always known what he was.

And now, I struggled with what I was.

Before me, Val lifted his head. His muscles had reknit. His bones cracked and remade.

He stood before me as the most magnificent, silvery-gray wolf I'd ever seen. His eyes glowed like sapphires. He took one step toward me then dropped his head.

Val. My protector. My beautiful wolf.

CHAPTER EIGHTEEN

WILLOW

I should have been scared. Terrified. Instead, it was as if all the jagged pieces of my life lined up and fit together.

Val was a wolf.

He came slowly toward me, dipping his head. I reached for him.

"There you are," I whispered. "You've been there all along, haven't you?"

He let out a keening wail, sidestepping.

I came closer. I sank my fingers into the soft fur between his ears. I ran my hand along his flank, feeling the powerful, corded muscles beneath.

His fur was a million colors. Silver, black, gray, even shades of brown. His tail twitched. He stomped the ground. His paws were massive. Even partially retracted, I could see the deadly curve to his claws.

Claw marks. I closed my eyes and imagined paws like these ripping across Val's back.

Val nuzzled my hand. I felt the sleek power of his back. And somehow, I still felt the man inside of him.

You're safe with me, Willow. You know I would never hurt you. I would die before I let anyone touch you without your consent again.

"I know," I said. I knelt down, cupping Val's snout in my hands. He licked his lips. He bared his fangs. I don't know what possessed me to do it, but I touched one. It was smooth as ivory, coming to a lethal point. He could rip a man to shreds in an instant. A shudder went through me. I knew I was safe with him, but another, horrifying truth slammed home.

Val swung his head, gesturing toward the bed.

You should sit. We have a lot to talk about.

I did as he commanded. Val went to the end of the bed. He squared off, facing me. Those brilliant, sapphire eyes of his flashed. Oh, God. I had been looking right at the truth this whole time. I'd seen his wolf eyes before. They glinted like that when his emotions ran high. When he was angry. When he was protective. When his desire rose.

He took a step back. That same whiff of magic filled the air, taking my breath away.

He bowed down. His neck grew long, straining. Then, one by one, his limbs grew. Bone and muscle snapped. In one, great, glorious breath, the wolf was gone and the man stood before me.

He was no less magnificent this way. So much beauty and power. Every muscle like chiseled granite. Strong, toned quads. Rippling abs.

He was naked. Lust coursed through me. He wanted me. And I wanted him.

I could hardly think straight. I wanted to run my fingers along his body like I'd done with the wolf. Strong, protective arms. He had carried me as if I weighed nothing. He had sliced through the water with the speed of a jet boat as I held on to his shoulder.

"Um," I said, my throat dry. "There's another robe in the bathroom."

Smiling, Val crossed the room and got it.

I sat with my hands folded as Val came out. He sat on the bed beside me.

"Are you scared?" he asked.

I shook my head. "I should be. But I'm not. Not of you."

"Good," he answered.

"Jason," I said, turning to him. "He's also a wolf. I saw it. I mean, I didn't really know what I was seeing. But, his face changed. I think he was trying to keep himself from...shifting."

"Probably," Val said. "He wants you."

My hand went to the back of my neck. "He tried to bite me."

"No. He threatened to bite you. He would not need to try."

I nodded. "I wanted it."

Val's jaw clenched.

"No," I said. "I mean I didn't want *him* to bite me there. But...I craved it."

"It's an Alpha's mark," he said. "When an Alpha wolf claims a mate, he bites her there. It seals a connection between them. He can sense her wherever she is. Becomes a part of her. And it goes the other way around too. The bond grows stronger with every bite."

My chest felt tight. "He wants to control me. That's what it means."

"No!" he said. Val took my hands in his. His skin was so hot. Electricity sparked between us.

"No," he said more softly. "Not control. That's not how it's supposed to be, Willow. A wolf's mate is supposed to choose for herself. It should never be done without consent."

"Except that's what Jason wants. You're not saying all of it,

Val. You're trying to protect me. But, I know. I don't know how, but I think I've always known. If Jason had marked me...like you say...I would have been bound to him. He'd make me want him even though I don't belong to him."

Val's voice turned low, more growl than human. "I will *never* let that happen. He'll have to kill me to get to you."

"But he's not alone. There are others. His men. They're wolves too. I heard them. I *saw* them. They're the ones who tortured you. You can't fight them all."

"You're never going back to that place. They'll never find you now. I told you Soren isn't the only one with powerful friends. He has a pack, yes. I don't. But I can protect you now that we're away from his territory."

"Those chains," I said.

"Dragonsteel," he answered. "They...they hold magic."

"You couldn't shift. You couldn't fight them off."

"And you set me free. It's over, Willow."

I leaped up from the bed. My heart raced. I wanted to run. I wanted to tear my hair out.

"I don't...God. Did my father know this the whole time?"

"I don't know."

"He was...Val, I overheard Jason a few days ago. A few of his...his pack were with him. The day I saw him with that key. It sounded like there was someone else he was working for. Someone else he answers to. He said...God, I wish I could remember it all. He said something about answering to the ring. I took it literally. He kept twirling that key ring and those...his wolves were staring at it. I thought he was hypnotizing them with it, as stupid as that sounds."

Val rose and stood beside me. He was calm. His eyes flashed as he took my hands.

"It's important," he said. "I don't know what it means. But, I need to run it by Payne, my boss. Soren is up to something that I think might be a serious threat to other shifters. That stall in the barn where they chained me? It's been there a while. The barn was built around it. I don't like that he had access to dragonsteel. We need to try and figure out why."

"Don't," I said. "Please don't tell Payne. He's on Jason's payroll too. I'm afraid of him. It's not over, Val. I saw Jason's eyes. He thinks I belong to him."

Val bared his teeth. I couldn't read his mind, but I could see his thoughts written plainly on his face. No. They were my thoughts too.

I didn't belong to Jason Soren. I belonged to Val.

I slipped my hands from his. My head spun.

"Willow," he said. "I meant what I said. I will *not* let that man come near you again. I need to keep you out of sight for now."

"No," I whispered. "You know what's going on, you're just not saying it."

"Willow, I have kept things from you. I won't deny that. But, everything I have told you is the truth."

"He let us go!" I blurted. It was as if Val turned to stone.

The moment I said it, it made as much sense as everything else.

"He did," I said. "How many men are in Jason's pack? Ten? Twenty? That place was crawling with them. I didn't understand what it was, but now I do. I could feel them. They were angry with him that he sent you to bring me to him. That's the other thing he said. I told you. He said he answers to the ring. Or maybe, the Ring. And whoever or whatever that is, they're the ones who wanted to involve your firm in all of this. He said you were just as important to him as I am."

Val ran a hand down his face. "That's good. Anything you can remember will help. And we *will* figure this out. I can promise you that."

"You haven't denied what I said, Val. Admit it. Jason totally just let us go. Why?"

He let out a sigh. Val sank to the bed again. When he finally looked up, his expression had turned grave.

"I don't know. That's the truth."

I sat beside him. Val took my hand.

"Willow," he said. "It's going to be okay. Somehow. You are

not going back to that man. No matter what. For now, just trust me. You should rest."

"Please don't patronize me, Val."

"I'm not. I swear. But, you're exhausted. We'll both think better after some rest."

I wanted to argue with him, but he was right. I was bone-tired. It hurt to think. And yet, it was so hard to let go.

"I'm not going anywhere," Val said, answering a question I hadn't even yet asked.

"You promise?"

His sad smile melted my heart. "On my life."

I touched his face. He turned and kissed my palm, sending a shiver of pleasure through me. I had so many more questions. No. That wasn't it. I had the answers. I just couldn't bring myself to say them just yet.

CHAPTER NINETEEN

VAL

"You need to let me call Payne."

I stood with my back to the kid at the front desk, my head buried in the booth of an honest to God pay phone. It was safer this way.

"Leo," I said. "This is how it's got to be for now."

"At least tell me where you are," he said.

"Look, you and the family are the only ones I trust right now. Soren's connections are deep. Payne's the one who sent me on this job."

"Payne is loyal to us, not Soren. There's no way Wolfguard would be in bed with a guy like that based on what you've said."

"And you've kept most of what I said to yourself." It was a statement and a question.

"Of course," Leo answered, irritated. "I'm just concerned about your judgment, Val. You were chained up in dragon-steel for how long?"

"Leo, it's complicated. This girl...Willow...she's special. She matters. I am not willing to take the chance that Wolfguard can't protect her like I can."

"Payne's one of the good guys, Val."

"I know. At least, I think so too. But until I know a little more, I want to do this my way."

Leo swore on the other end of the phone. I knew I'd be asking the same questions if this conversation were happening the other way around. But, Willow's safety was too damn important. I trusted myself. I trusted my family.

"At least let me call Uncle Andre," Leo said. "You need backup."

"My brother can't do much for me in Moscow. The minute he starts making waves down here, I have a hunch Soren will figure it out. I'm in the middle of nowhere. He's never going to find her. I just need you to do what you promised. Get in touch with Payne. Arrange a meeting. Two days. Then get your ass down here or send Milo or Erik or Edward if you can't."

"I don't like it," he said.

"I know."

Leo knew it was no use arguing with me. I would meet with Payne in person, far away from Willow, while one of my nephews watched over her. On the off chance Payne or Wolfguard itself had been compromised, it was the best way to keep her safe.

"Just check in," Leo said. "I want to hear from you every couple of hours."

"I'll try." Then, I hung up the phone.

It was well past midnight. After a vending machine dinner, Willow had finally fallen asleep.

I made my way back to the room. A full moon rose high. I scanned the gas station parking lot across the street. There were two minivans filling up and a handful of drunks inside the convenience store. I overheard the desk clerk say the motel was vacant except for three rooms, mine and two on the other end of the building.

I grabbed another cup of complimentary, shitty coffee and went back to Willow.

She stirred a little, rolling to her side as I closed the door. She slept curled in on herself, her lips in a pout. Her hair fanned out behind her.

Leo had wired me some cash. I bought some essentials at the truck stop. Willow sported an oversized, "Virginia is for Lovers" t-shirt.

I sat on the chair next to the bed and watched her. The steady rise and fall of her chest calmed me. Her brow furrowed. She was dreaming.

Her lips parted and her tongue darted out. I set my coffee down. Her hair had fallen over her eye. I reached for her and gently smoothed it back.

She was so beautiful. Strong. Scared, but brave. Even when she couldn't possibly know the danger she'd been in, she went up against Soren and stole the key to free me.

I clenched my jaw, imagining how close she had come to being marked by him.

Willow rolled to her back. Her t-shirt rode up and the sheet had fallen away, exposing her cotton panties and her bare stomach.

I tried to tear my eyes away. I wanted to lick my way down the flat planes of her stomach, around her perfect belly button. I wanted to give her pleasure like she'd never known.

My wolf stirred. I tried to focus on baseball. Harsh Siberian winters. Anything.

I picked up the empty Styrofoam coffee cup and crushed.

Willow moaned. Her hips moved. Her skin flushed. She fisted the sheet, still caught in her dream. She began to gyrate.

Fuck.

It was a sex dream. I rose from my chair and staggered toward the window.

"Val!" she cried out. I froze.

Was she dreaming about me? I wasn't sure I could stay in the same room with her a second longer. Her scent changed as her arousal grew. Oh, God. It lured me. Intoxicated me. I gripped the door handle.

"Val," she said again, breathless.

Straightening my back, I turned to her. Her hair wild, Willow sat upright in bed, clutching the sheet around her.

"You're safe," I said. "It was just a dream."

She nodded, licked her lips. Her legs were unsteady as she rose from the bed and came to me.

She was still aroused. She tried to force a smile. The woman had no idea how her scent acted on me. I could *feel* the heat between her legs.

"You left," she said. "I woke up a little while ago and you weren't here."

"Just making a phone call from the lobby," I said. "I didn't go far."

She tilted her head. "I know. I mean...I don't know how I knew, but I did. I could kind of, I don't know, sense you."

She put a hand on my arm. It was kinetic energy between

us. She was still so hot. Her desire thrummed through her, intensifying the pulse between her legs.

It was everything. It was too much. Her lust stirred mine. I grew hard in an instant.

"Willow," I said, my voice choked. "I need to get some air."

"Don't," she said, gasping. She put her other hand on me, turning me away from the window.

It was lightning. Fire. The most intense heat and urge I'd ever felt. This could end only one of three ways. Either I put some distance between us and got a hold of myself. Or I would shift right there. Or...

"I know what I am," she whispered. "I dreamt it."

"Willow, you can't possibly..."

"I do," she said. "I've known it from the minute I met you. I think before, even."

"Willow..."

"I trust you," she said. "And I want..."

"Willow..."

I was losing control. Her touch. Her breath. Her heady scent as lust burned through her. It burned through me.

"Listen to me," she said. "I know what I want. And I want you. Right here. Right now."

She took a step back. My heart burned for her. I stood rigid. Ready. I couldn't breathe.

Willow lifted her t-shirt, pulled it over her head, and threw it in the corner of the room. She stood before me in nothing but those white, cotton panties. Goosebumps covered her flesh. Her breasts were round, soft, supple. Her wine-colored nipples darkened with her arousal.

"Val," she said, coming back to me. She put a hand on my chest, right over my heart. When she felt it, she let out a little gasp. She knew. She felt what I did. My heart pounded in perfect synchrony with her own. We were two halves of one whole. Or...we could be if she was willing to give in to it. "I was...we were made for this...weren't we?" she asked.

God. She knew all along. I spent so much time trying to figure out how to explain to her what I was. What we were. It was a waste of time. She knew. She was born knowing.

"What Jason tried to do to you," I started, then hated myself for bringing that monster's name into this moment.

"You're not Jason," she said. "You're...mine.'"

"Yes."

"So take me. I want you to. I need you to."

"Willow, you don't understand what you're asking of me."

"I'm not asking you. I'm telling you. This is what I want. Don't you get it? I've spent my whole life trying to be what other people thought I should be. I've tried to mold myself into what my father wanted. I've tried to pretend who my father really was didn't matter. And even Jason. At first, he was a way for me to escape. Then, he was a way for me to help my family. He was never for me. It was never about me. But this, this is. This is everything. You're everything. And I think...I think I love you."

I *knew* I loved her.

"Please," she said. She hooked her thumbs under the waistband of her panties and cast those aside too.

She was naked, gorgeous, and offering herself to me.

I touched her. Her whole body quivered with pleasure as I gently rolled her nipple with my thumb.

"I want to taste you," I said.

"Then do it. Please, Val. Do it all."

Her hands were on my fly. I cupped her head with my hand and brought my lips down to hers.

She tasted like heaven as her lips parted. I teased her with my tongue, loving the way she groaned in my mouth.

Sugar. Cinnamon. Honey. She was every sweet flavor and others I couldn't name. She was Willow. She was mine.

I sprung free in her gentle hands. It was my turn to groan as she stroked me. I wanted that. I wanted her mouth. I wanted her sweet pussy. I wanted it all.

"Your eyes," she whispered, bringing a hand to my face. "They're so beautiful. Your wolf eyes."

I knew they blazed strong as my lust heightened.

I wrapped an arm around her waist and lifted her. Willow let out a squeal as I swept her off her feet and carried her to the bed.

I laid her down gently, knowing it was the last gentle thing I would do. She sensed it. Her eyes gave off a glint of their own as her legs fell open, beckoning me.

"I can't go slow, once we start," I said.

She arched her back. "Thank God!"

I pressed her knees flat against the bed, spreading her wide. Her little sex pulsed for me. She was already soaked.

I ran my tongue down her thigh, loving the way she squirmed in anticipation. I gave her little nips that made her gasp. She arched her back, straining to her keep her legs wide open as an offer.

I settled between her legs. My craving for her reached a fever pitch. I licked along her sweet folds, teasing my way around her clit.

"Val!" she screamed out.

"Patience, baby," I said.

She bucked, losing control. Willow was my wild thing. I would take her to the edge and back.

I suckled her. The taste of her ignited my soul. She was the lock. I was the key. She opened for me, set me free.

She went beyond words. She thrust her hips as I lapped at her. I hooked three fingers together and slid them into her slick opening. She fucked me with abandon, craving so much more.

"Please, Val," she found her words to beg again.

I wished I had rope. I wanted nothing more than to tie her to the bed, spread eagle for me so I could take my time and relish the way she squirmed and begged.

"You're so beautiful," I whispered, coming up for air. I stood up and stoked myself. A tiny bead of liquid formed at the tip. Willow saw it. She rose up, slid her hands around my buttocks and licked me.

My knees buckled as she wrapped her lips around me. It was my turn to be tortured.

I threaded my fingers through her hair, driving her down on me. She met me thrust for thrust, working me with expert skill. She knew just how much pressure to use. Just how to draw me out.

My eyes rolled in the back of my head. I was so close to letting go.

"Not yet," she whispered, popping off of me.

"Get on your back," I said.

She complied. Willow scrambled to the head of the bed

and spread her legs for me again. I went up on my knees between her thighs.

"Are you sure?" I said, even though I already knew the answer.

"More than I've ever been about anything."

And then, I couldn't hold back a second longer.

I plunged into her. I meant to ease my way, but once her lips opened for me, I had to have all of her. Willow grabbed my shoulders, bracing herself as I took her deep.

She slid down further on the bed, bringing her knees up almost to her ears. I pushed her thighs out. She was impossibly wide. I was impossibly deep.

God. She felt so good. Pulsing heat. She gushed around me. So wet. So perfect. Made for me.

I braced my feet against the headboard and pressed into her as far as I could go. I froze, letting Willow take up the rhythm. She dug her nails into my back, drawing blood. I let out a growl that made the windows vibrate.

She came. In thunderous, crashing waves. She threw her head back and arched her whole body. I felt the electric vibrations take over her. She came hard and deep and screaming out my name.

I stayed stock still, letting her take all she needed from me. On and on she thrust until sweat beaded her brow and plastered her hair to her face.

Then, finally, she crested down. I felt her release with a quiet sigh as her legs turned to rubber.

"My God," she whispered. "I don't think I can move."

"Yes you can, baby. You can take so much more. Get up on your hands and knees."

Her eyes snapped wide. A new flush of pleasure colored her cheeks as she realized what I was about to do.

Her movements were sluggish, but she did as she was told. She gripped the headboard and went up on her knees.

God. The sight of her like that. Open. Still so wet for me.

I stroked myself again then got in position. I thrust into her as I gripped her hips to guide the way. Willow's head dropped against the headboard. She sagged into the movements. Her arms trembled. Her body rocked as I worked her.

Then, I let go. I threw my head back and howled as I filled Willow and took my release.

She sated me for a moment, but I knew I would only crave her more once we started.

Willow stayed in position even as her knees trembled with fatigue.

Minutes slipped by. Hours. Over and over, I brought her back to the brink of pleasure and beyond.

I took her from the bed, to the floor. She followed me into

SHIFT OF FATE   195

the shower and I fucked her there too. I made her mine as the sun finally began to peek through the slats in the blinds. I lost count of how many times I took her that night.

Then, in the quiet, as she spooned against me. Willow pulled her hair to the side.

It happened so naturally. She didn't say anything. I'm not even sure if she made a conscious choice. But, in her heart and soul she was a wolf's mate. My fated mate. Her body demanded what her mind hadn't yet named.

She moved, going on all fours again. She dropped her head and let her hair fall back to the side. I was still inside of her.

My primal nature took over. I wanted to ask her if she was sure of this too. But, I was beyond words.

"Yes," she gasped, already knowing my mind. "I want this too. I love you, Val."

I licked the back of her neck. She would have me mark her. Right here. Right now. She knew what it meant.

Part of me wanted to find the strength to draw back. We hadn't had a conversation about this. I told her what Soren tried to do. I didn't talk about how it was really supposed to be between two fated mates. It turned out, I didn't need to. My Willow understood.

I grazed her neck with my teeth. My wolf rose.

"Yes!" she gasped again. "Do it! Oh, God. Oh, Val!"

I reared back. I knew what she felt because I felt it through her. She experienced a pulsation at the base of her neck like a brand new erogenous zone. She would taste oh, so sweet as I marked her as mine forever.

I leaned in. I let my fangs drop. I tasted her skin and felt her blood rising to the surface.

Then, a bolt of lightning went through me, rocking me backward. Pain seared off the top of my head. My heart exploded. I clutched my chest and rolled off of her.

I was outside my body. I saw myself through Willow's eyes as I twitched on the ground.

"Val!" Willow's scream reached me as if I were underwater. I was drowning. I was spinning through space.

Then, my lungs exploded and there was blackness all around.

CHAPTER TWENTY

WILLOW

"Val!"

He couldn't hear me. He writhed on the ground, shifting from wolf to man then stuck in between. His eyes were wild, blood red. I couldn't get through to him.

The worst of it was, I felt his pain. Each breath he took sent stabbing agony through his whole body. He clawed at the air, the ground, me, anything.

"Val," I said, trying to keep my own panic from rising. He hadn't marked me. I had craved it more than anything in my life. I could *feel* the pleasure of his bite. It would complete a circle. My whole life had been leading up to that moment. I knew it in my heart.

But, the moment Val's teeth scraped the sensitive flesh at the back of my neck, I felt the lightning storm inside of him.

"Val, please." I willed myself calm. Instinct told me the more afraid I was, the worse it was for him. I also knew that if he *had* bitten me, whatever afflicted him might have killed me.

He settled a bit as I did. I sat on the ground, bracing my back against the footboard. With great effort, I pulled Val to me, cradling his head in my lap. I sang to him. Soothing sounds. I rubbed his temple and kissed his cheek.

Slowly. Painfully. He came back to me. His body went slack. He took one great, heaving breath. His claws retracted. His eyes went from red to blue. He shuddered, then came back into himself.

Sweat poured down his back. His skin was almost colorless. But, he looked up and met my eyes.

"Val," I said, crying out.

He reached up and touched my cheek. "There you are," he whispered.

"I'm right here. Baby. What happened to you?"

He put a hand to his head. He pulled himself up until he sat beside me.

"Are you all right? Did I hurt you?"

"No," I said. "I'm fine. But, what was that?"

"I don't know," he answered. "God help me. I don't know."

"You were about to bite me. To mark me. I wanted you to. I

still want you to. Then, I don't know. You had some sort of attack. A seizure."

His color got better. The trembling in his hands stopped. He ran his fingers through his hair. He got to his feet and found his pants.

"That's never happened to me before," he said.

"Val, you need help. If you're sick."

"I'm not sick. Wolf shifters don't get sick like that unless there's magic involved or..."

"Or what?"

"Mating sickness," he said. "I think it's worse for bears, but if an Alpha goes too long without finding his mate, it gets harder to stay in control. But that's not what that was."

"Well, we were mating. Maybe..."

"No," he said. "It would be the opposite. Mating is the cure for mating sickness. It's not the other way around."

"Magic then," I said, rising to my feet. I slipped on my panties and a tank top. "Maybe Jason did something to you."

"My skin's crawling," he said. Sure enough, he scratched at his arms then tried to reach his back.

I went to him. I ran my fingers over his flesh. He felt a little cooler to the touch than usual. Val's wolf blood normally made him run hot.

"He hurt you here, and here." I touched his shoulders, his cheek, all the places where the claw marks had been the worst. They were all healed now.

"Maybe it was that dragonsteel?" I asked. "You were in it for days. Can you get sick from it?"

"I don't think so. Not permanently, anyway. I mean, shifters can't break through it. And...it made it so I couldn't shift while I was bound. I've heard it's like that with cages made of the stuff. But, it doesn't have any lasting effect."

"What about the men you work for? Mr. Fallon, you said. You've checked in, right?"

Val's eyes darkened. "Not yet. It's better if nobody knows where to find us. Especially now."

He squirmed, pulling at the skin on his shoulders.

"Stop that," I said. "Come in the bathroom with me where the light is better."

He was still clawing at himself as we stood in front of the vanity. I made him sit with his back to the mirror.

I trailed my fingers down his arms, looking for any sign of a wound or a rash. His skin was red from scratching, but looked normal.

"The pain you felt," I said. "Can you localize it?"

There were only the faintest red marks on his back where Jason's wolves had torn him up. In another day or two, those would be all but healed.

I felt a burning sensation at the base of my neck. That same craving pulled at me. Being this close to Val and not having him touch me, not having him inside of me was starting to get to me.

I pushed every lust-filled thought I had to the back of my brain. My hand flew absently to the base of my neck as if covering it would make the craving less urgent.

My heart raced.

"What is it?" he asked, immediately sensing the shift in my mood. God, how good would it have felt to have had him finish the marking so I could connect with him all the way?

"Turn your head," I said. I brushed the hair away from his neck, searching for the spot on him that burned on me.

"There," I said, gasping.

I almost missed it. If I hadn't been so close to him in the harsh light, I never would have seen it.

"Willow?"

"It's so tiny," I said. It was. High on Val's left shoulder, almost at the base of his neck, he still had the tiniest mark.

He brought his fingers up. I took his hand and guided him to the scar I saw.

"Is it a bite?"

I moved so my head didn't block the light.

"No," I answered. "It's a straight line. I mean, it's hardly more than a paper cut. It's just...I've seen gashes on your skin twenty times as thick heal overnight."

"That wasn't there before," Val said, his voice dropping to that low growl.

I pressed my thumbs to the edges of the mark. I couldn't really call it a wound. It was far too faint.

It took a few tries. I had to hold my breath and go very still. But, sure enough, as I pressed on the sides of the mark, I could feel the outline of a hard lump underneath. Once again, I guided Val's fingers to the back of his neck so he could feel what I felt.

He went rigid. His wolf eyes flashed. I felt his pulse thunder through him.

"Willow," he said, his tone grave. "I need you to get a knife. I need you to cut it out."

I pulled my hand away as if his skin seared mine. "You're crazy! I don't even know what it is."

"I don't either. But, I know it's not part of me. You asked me to localize my pain. It was the right question. Because it started right here at the base of my neck. Like an electric shock."

"I know," I said, taking a step away from him. "I...I felt it too. Through you."

"Soren did something to me. I was in that barn for days. A lot of it I don't remember. He had the opportunity..."

"He let us go," I said, panic rising. "This is why."

Val slowly nodded. "He tried to turn me."

"What do you mean, turn you?"

Val ran a hard hand through his hair. "Subjugation. Alpha wolves can subjugate less powerful betas and omegas into their pack."

"Like mind control?"

"No," he said sharply. "No. Not mind control. A good Alpha is a man who betas and omegas *want* to follow. They do it willingly. They're loyal. But subjugation allows the pack to communicate telepathically. It allows them to move as one unit if there's a danger to the pack."

"And he wanted you to be part of his pack," I said. "But you're not a beta."

"No," he said. "He tried anyway. He failed."

"Jason wants me for himself. He knew what you were. You think he put...whatever that thing is in you so you wouldn't try to mark me?"

"I don't know. Maybe."

"If he didn't want you to have me, why the hell didn't he just kill you if he had the chance?"

"I don't know," Val said, growling again. He moved past me back into the main room. He went to the table near the window and rifled through the grocery bags he brought back the other day from the gas station convenience store. He pulled out a Swiss army knife from a plastic package and handed it to me.

"What do you need that for?" I asked.

"I bought it for you. It was the only thing remotely resembling a weapon you can buy next to a display of corn nuts, Willow."

He handed it to me. The blade glinted.

Val came back under the harsh lights of the vanity mirror and exposed his neck.

"Cut it out," he commanded.

"Val, you need a doctor. I can't just carve into you here. It's not sanitary. What if I cut something...er...you need?"

"You won't," he said. "I'm an Alpha wolf, Willow. We're harder to kill than that. You'd have to shoot me directly through the heart and be damn lucky. Unless that blade is made of dragonsteel or you think I'd hold still long enough for you to cut off my damn head with it, you can't kill me. Anything you do to me will heal, just like the slash marks from Soren's pack."

"We don't know what that thing is," I said, my voice rising high, almost hysterical. "We don't know what it's connected to. No...we *do* know. It's your central nervous system. I saw what it did to you. How do you know it's not built with some kind of...of kill switch?"

"We don't," Val said. He turned and looked me straight in the eye.

"Val...please..."

"Willow, I will not go another second with that thing inside of me. I can feel it. If I could claw it out of me, I would. I just...I don't think it'll let me. It has to be you."

He turned and braced himself, gripping the sink. He dropped his head, exposing the back of his neck.

"Shit," I said.

"I know. Just commit. And be quick. I told you, you can't kill me."

"Right. Doesn't mean it won't hurt like hell!"

"You're right," he said. He stormed back to the main room and grabbed a bottle of bourbon from the grocery bag. He unscrewed the cap and drank deep.

"Give me that," I said.

Val raised a brow. "I think one of us should have a clear head."

I took the bottle. "It's not for my head. It's for the knife." I poured some alcohol over the blade. Val nodded and got back into position.

"Shit," I said again. Then, I took a shot.

Val gripped the sink so hard he cracked the porcelain. I

took a steadying breath, pressed the hard knot with my thumb and forefinger, then sliced just below it.

Val grimaced. He ground his teeth. But, he stayed still as stone as I worked the knife through.

I tried not to think too hard about what I was doing. I felt the hard edge of metal. I slipped the point of the blade beneath it.

Mercifully, the thing came out with a pop. Slick with Val's blood, it was a hard, black disk about the size of a quarter. I held it in my palm as Val straightened.

Wolf shifters might be impervious to being stabbed in the neck, but they sure did bleed a lot. He pressed a hand towel to his neck and it became soaked red in a matter of seconds.

Val took the disk from me and held it under the light.

"What is it?" I asked.

"I have no idea. But...shit..."

"What?" I asked. I felt Val's alarm. His pulse quickened.

"Whatever it is," he said. "It's uh...beeping. Can't you hear it?"

I did then. Just a tiny, barely perceptible sound. But, it was there. A rhythmic beep like when a smoke detector battery is about to go out.

"What about you?" I asked. "Do you feel anything different?"

He rolled his shoulder and took the towel away. The wound I made was angry and jagged, but the edges of it were already starting to reknit. The bleeding had stopped.

"Just stings a little."

"Val," I said. The hair on the back of my own neck started to rise.

"What?" He froze, sensing the change in me.

"It's just..." I backed out of the bathroom. I found my jeans and t-shirt. "I just think it's time to get out of here."

"I think you're right," Val said. He stood beside me.

The next sound went through me with the force of a gunshot.

A low, keening howl. Then another. And another after that.

Val ran to the window and peeled back the curtain.

"Fuck," he whispered.

"What is it?"

Val let the curtain drop. When he turned to me, his wolf eyes flashed bright.

"It's Soren's pack," he said. "They found us. We're surrounded."

CHAPTER TWENTY-ONE

VAL

My growl was a low vibration. I curled my fist and watched my claws come out. Pairs of yellow eyes glittered and swung back and forth as Soren's wolves took their position around the perimeter of the motel.

"Val," Willow said behind me.

I wanted to tell her it was going to be okay. But, I knew this would only end in death.

"How many?" she asked.

"I don't know for sure. He had a least a dozen that I saw back at the compound. There might have been more hiding in the woods."

"A dozen. Plus Jason. You can't take on thirteen at once. Val, we need help."

There was no help to come. That was my fault. I wasn't ready to trust Wolfguard. I wasn't willing to put my nephews in harm's way until I knew what I was dealing with.

Well, now I knew.

"I led them here," I said, my words leaving a bitter taste in my mouth. I held the black disk in my hand. "There must be a tracker in it."

I punched the wall. My nostrils flared.

"Val, stop," Willow said. She grabbed my arm. "You won't do us any good if you go feral on me. We have to think. Jason wants something. He could have killed you a hundred different times back in that barn. You're right. He let us get away. It means there's still room to negotiate. We can stall for time."

She was logical. I was predatory. I knew what Soren wanted. He wanted Willow. He wanted to torture me.

"Let me try to talk to him," she said. "Jason isn't going to hurt me."

"He's going to mark you!" I growled. "He probably wants to make me watch."

"So you do it!" she yelled. "If you mark me first, he can't, right?"

"It's not that simple," I said.

"It is. That chip is out of you. There's nothing stopping us.

Val, I won't go with him. I can't. I'd rather die than let him touch me again."

"If he gets a hold of you, even after I mark you, he can mark you himself. I can't protect you that way."

Willow sank to the bed. God. I'd failed her. I'd made her a single promise, to protect her. Now, I couldn't keep it.

"Then, we stall for time, just like I said. I don't care what Jason is. He's also a man living in the world. His family business relies on alliances like the one he's trying to form with my father. That's still true. My father has to be worried sick about me. Jason made him a promise to look after me. So let me lie to him. Let me tell him I'll go with him but not until he lets me talk to my dad first."

Again, she made sense. And again, I felt my feral side coming out. I wanted blood. I wanted to feel Jason Soren's life leeching out of him at my hands. Because I knew exactly what he wanted with Willow. I felt his need when he tried to get inside my head. And I'd underestimated him.

"Kalenkov!"Jason's shout echoed across the parking lot.

"He needs an alliance with your family too," Willow said. "Am I right? I told you I overheard him saying you were just as important to him as I am. You said your brother is head of a powerful pack in Moscow. What do you think he'll do to Jason when he finds out what he's trying to do to us?"

"They won't do me a lot of good five thousand miles away."

"We have to try," she said. "If you won't go out there and talk to him, I will. We can't fight our way out of this. We have no choice."

"Kalenkov, either you come out willingly, or I send them in after you."

To punctuate his point, Soren's wolves let out a chorus of howls that sent a chill through me. I could detect thirteen distinct voices. So it was fourteen against one. I could handle four or five of the betas on my own. Not thirteen.

"Val," Willow said. I was already only my feet and heading toward the door.

"Don't come out," I said. "No matter what you hear."

She had the Swiss army knife in her hand. It wouldn't do her a bit of good. Even a beta wolf was far too powerful for her to fight off.

"I'm going with you," she said.

I snapped my teeth. "Stay. Here. If you come out there with me, I'm going to shift. I won't be able to stop myself. Soren will see it as an act of aggression."

She sank to the bed. "Oh, God. Val. Be careful."

I took a breath and opened the door. I shielded Willow from view with my body and closed the door.

Jason stood behind four of his largest betas. The others formed a wall around the motel, cutting off any line of escape. I couldn't see them all, but I could sense at least four on the other side of the building. The thought occurred to me to punch a damn hole in the wall and take Willow out through it. There was now no chance of that working either. The only way past Soren, was through him.

"It's over, Kalenkov," Soren said. "You're beaten. If it makes you feel any better, you're smarter than I thought you were. Valiant, even. But you know this only ends one of two ways."

"What's your play?" I asked.

Soren's brow went up a fraction of an inch.

"You'd be an asset to the pack. I'd make you my second in command. You'd have your own territory in northern Virginia. Money. Power. Any mate you want. Except for Willow. She belongs to me."

"You know what I am," I said. "And if it's an alliance you want with my family, this is the wrong way to go about it."

"You're an Alpha," he said. "I'll admit, that surprised me. With Andre Kalenkov as your brother, I just assumed you weren't. That was my one mistake."

"Just the one?"

Soren smiled. "Fair enough. But I'm offering you more than you're getting from your brother. You have no place in the Kalenkov pack with him in charge. And Wolfguard? You're just a worker bee there and you know it. I'm offering you real power. A stake in something big. If you'd look past your own ego for two seconds, you'd see I'm right. Why do you think I asked Payne Fallon for you special? This doesn't have to be so...epic."

"Oh," I said taking a step toward him. "I think it does."

His wolves bared their teeth. Soren put a hand up to quiet them.

"You may not know it, but our families already do go way back. My mother's family was in Russia before there were Kalenkovs. A thousand years ago. Our families were allies then. We can be allies again. It's for the good of all of us."

"I doubt my brother thinks so," I said.

Soren raised that brow again. "You sure about that?"

My step faltered for a second. He seemed so sure of himself. My heart and thoughts raced. Did Andre already know what was happening?

No. Soren was trying to get under my skin.

"I won't lie to you," I said. "I'm not cut out to follow another Alpha."

It was in me to remind him he already knew that. But, as it stood, I figured I had exactly one advantage. Soren had no idea I'd already ripped out the chip he put in my neck. Let him be cocky. Let him think he could control me anyway with a single press of a button or however the hell he controlled that thing.

If I got close enough. If I had the element of surprise. Because that was the one thing I hadn't told Willow. If I got close enough to Soren to break his neck, it would only take me an instant to do it. Then, his pack would be in disarray. With me being the only Alpha around, I could subjugate them myself. It was a long shot. Dangerous as fuck. But, I saw no other alternative.

"Maybe there's another way," I said. "I do have influence with my brother. And he *is* looking for ways to expand the pack here. If our families go way back like you say, then you already know what we've had to overcome to take pack power in the motherland. Andre never wants to be vulnerable like that again. You can never be my Alpha. You knew that was off the table. But, I can be something else."

Soren's lip curled into a smile. I took another step closer. If I couldn't get those wolves to break their line in front of him, this would never work.

As long as Jason thought he had the chip to his advantage, he might let his guard down long enough to shake my hand.

"I'll partner with you," I said. "In spite of everything. But, I have my own price."

The black wolf at Soren's left growled low. The hair on his back went up in a ridge.

"You're bargaining with me now?"

"I am. You have something I want."

Soren looked back toward the motel room. I didn't dare follow his line of sight. If Willow met my eyes, she might figure out what I was doing. Or she might distract me without meaning to.

"Dragonsteel," I said. "I want to know where you got it. Last I heard, nobody could get their hands on the stuff anymore."

"Now, what would you want with dragonsteel?"

I gritted my teeth. "Let's just say I've got some scores still to settle on behalf of my family. And I know some people who might pay a pretty hefty price to get their hands on more of it."

I took another step toward Soren. I was no more than a foot away from his closest wolves.

"Just dragonsteel?" he asked.

"The source of your dragonsteel...and the girl. That's my price. You give me that, you have your partnership. You have your alliance with the Russian pack."

Slowly, carefully, I reached out and offered Jason Soren my hand. I could feel his wolves' breath on my wrist. My fangs dropped. I kept my jaw clamped shut to keep him from seeing.

"Willow's mine," he said. "She was part of another bargain my family struck long before she was even born."

"She's not yours," I said. "You know she's my fated mate. You sensed it. And because of it, you also know she's a deal breaker for me. You're a smart man, Jason. Cunning, even. If I told you anything else, you'd know I was lying."

This got a genuine laugh out of him. "You're right. But you're also out of luck. Willow stays with me. Never mind what I paid for her. She's how I know you'll fall in line."

His words lit a fuse in me. What he paid for her? She was nothing more than a commodity to him. He would use her against me as long as he lived. As long as I lived.

At that moment, I knew one thing with total clarity. Jason Soren would never stop trying to collect whatever debt he felt he was owed for Willow. The only way to keep her safe was if Soren was dead.

My life no longer mattered. My pain no longer mattered. Willow was my fated mate and I would protect her no matter what.

An instant. A movement. A flash of fangs. I would rip Jason Soren's throat out and taste his blood as he died. I would die with him, but it was the only way Willow would be truly free.

Soren saw something in my eyes. I saw the same in his. We were done talking.

He slipped a hand in his pocket. When he took it out, he held something small and black in his palm. He pressed it with his thumb.

A transmitter?

There was no other time but now. I lunged for him, breaking through his line of wolves.

Soren's eyes went wide as I landed with the full weight of my body on his chest.

I felt fangs ripping into my back as his wolves moved to protect their Alpha. I bit down, tearing at Jason's neck.

The wolves were everywhere, pulling me back. Behind me, Willow screamed.

I existed outside myself. I saw her running toward me. Two wolves blocked her path, their fangs dripping. Their eyes filled with bloodlust.

Too late.

I tasted death. I tasted failure.

Soren rolled to his side as six wolves descended on me. The weight of them crushed my ribs. Three more came in from the side.

Now it was nine wolves, dragging me by my legs and tail away from Soren.

I tried to fight them off. I tried to scream. I had no voice. I had only feral rage as I fought for my life and the life of my mate

Soren gave the command. I felt it reverberate through his pack of wolves.

Kill!

It wouldn't be over quickly. They would tear me limb from limb, but it would be Soren who took the death blow.

Then, a blur of movement came from the side. Two of Jason's wolves rolled off me, yelping as they scattered.

I sank my fangs into another wolf, immobilizing him.

Somehow, I got up. My head swung low, my vision doubled.

I wasn't part of a pack. But, my family bond was strong.

My nephew Milo's wolf grabbed one of Soren's by the neck and flung him against the side of the motel.

My nephew Leo took out the two wolves closest to Willow. She staggered backward and pressed herself against the motel room door.

Erik and Edward flanked the wolves around the perimeter. Soren had the numbers, but each of my four nephews was a full-blooded Siberian Alpha wolf. Soren's betas were outmatched.

Milo brought friends. A bear shifter barreled down on Soren himself. He scrambled back.

Then, the twin tigers came. They took on the three wolves left standing as they tried to protect their Alpha.

I got to my feet. I headed straight for Soren. The bear and tigers cleared the way. We weren't pack. We weren't even the same species. But, these were the men of Wolfguard. We were brothers in our own way.

I towered over Soren's wolf.

He shifted. He sat up, putting his hands in front of his face.

"Kalenkov, stop," he said. "This will go worse for you than for me. You have no idea the ripple effect you're starting."

I snapped my teeth. The tigers held their ground over Soren's wolves. He hadn't yet given them the command to stand down and shift.

I shifted. I knelt beside Soren as he leaned against the tire of a Jeep parked beside him.

"You're not as smart as you think you are," I said.

"You work for me!" he shouted. "All of you. I bought and paid for Wolfguard protection. When word gets out you bit the hand that feeds you, none of you will be safe. You tell that to Payne Fallon."

"Who do you think sent us here, you asshole!" This from the bear shifter. He was huge and broad like all bears were. He had an unruly mass of brown hair and that characteristic "bear" smell. He had hands roughly the size of dinner plates and he held one of Soren's wolves up by the scruff of his neck.

"Game over," I said to Soren.

Willow was at my side. "Where's my father?" she asked, breathless. In all the chaos, I hadn't thought to ask about him. Willow was right to be worried. There was no telling how Soren reacted when we left the party. Still part of me didn't care. Soren's words reverberated. He paid for her. Paid whom? Rousseau?

"He'll go to prison now, Willow," Jason said. "It'll be on your head."

"It's on his," she said. "He never would have tried to buy his freedom with me."

"He can't protect you like I can," Soren said. "Kalenkov is nothing but a hired gun. He has no real power."

Willow looked around the parking lot. Every one of Soren's wolves was backed into a corner by one of my nephews or another member of Wolfguard.

"Looks pretty powerful to me," she said. "And Val's power comes naturally, Jason. He didn't take it by coercion or this." She opened her palm to reveal the tiny black disk she held in it.

Soren's eyes changed, going from amber to red.

No!

He lunged for Willow. He gave a single command.

Die!

Every one of Soren's wolves obeyed. They had no choice. They went after the men of Wolfguard. They never stood a chance.

I grabbed Soren himself as he tried to complete his shift.

Willow fell backward. The disk skipped across the parking lot.

Soren and I met midair. Wolf against wolf. I sank my fangs into his neck, shredding his jugular.

He was dead before he hit the ground.

Adrenaline coursed through me. I shifted and got to my feet. I dove for Willow. She was safe, unharmed. She flung her arms around me as I tried to pull her away from the carnage.

"Wait," she gasped.

She bent down and picked up the disk. It had wedged against the back tire of the parked Jeep.

She held it up. I put my arm around her.

It was then that Leo got to us. Sweat plastered his dark hair to his forehead.

"What was that?" he asked. His eyes traveled to the tiny black circle Willow once again held in her palm.

"Something he was willing to die for," she said, looking at Jason Soren's lifeless form.

I held her close. I knew I would never let her go.

My eyes met Leo's. I had a thousand questions. Only one thing mattered.

"Thank you," I said. "How did you know to come? I told you not to."

Leo smiled. "Well, you've always been a stubborn son of a bitch. And somehow I also knew you were wrong."

"Thank God," I said.

I let Willow go long enough to hug Leo. I thumped his back.

"So who's this?" Milo asked as we broke.

I smiled. "Leo, meet Willow. She's...my mate."

Willow extended a hand. "It's good to meet you," she said.

"Nah," Leo said, pulling Willow into a hug. "She's more than that. I can tell. Welcome to the family."

CHAPTER TWENTY-TWO

WILLOW

TWO WEEKS LATER...

ALPINE, NEW JERSEY

I sat on the back porch, sipping lemonade. Spring had given way to summer and the hot sun warmed my face. A perfect day. The smell of freshly cut grass filled my head. A white and yellow butterfly landed on the porch swing beside me then took flight as soon as the shouting started again.

Lisette hadn't stopped screaming since she came downstairs. Before that, she tried crying. Next, she'd probably start throwing dishes. That wouldn't last long. My father's bodyguards kept a respectable distance, but they'd never let her come anywhere near him.

I took another sip of lemonade.

"Miss Rousseau?" Calvin Mulroney, my father's personal secretary, poked his head out. "You bags are in the front hallway. Your car is about ten minutes out. I know things are...um...disorganized inside, but your father wanted to make sure you checked in with him before you left."

"Thanks, Calvin," I said, setting down my glass. I rose, steeled myself for the onslaught I knew I faced, then headed back into the house.

Lisette's face had turned a grisly purple. Her nostrils flared and her chest heaved when she saw me. My father sat stoic at the head of the dining room table.

"You have no idea what you've done," Lisette railed. "Look around. All of this. They'll take it all!"

My father's two hulking bodyguards stood in the hallway, ready to intervene if Lisette made her way to the China cabinet.

"It's not her fault," my father said calmly. "Now, if you don't mind, I'm going to take a few minutes to talk to my daughter."

"Fine," Lisette said, folding her hands. "Can't wait to hear what she has to say for herself this time."

My father cleared his throat and gestured to his body-guards. They stepped forward. Lisette swore as she realized what that all meant.

Thankfully, she stormed out of the room, leaving nothing but the echo of curse words in her wake.

"When are you leaving?" Dad asked.

"Ten minutes or so," I said.

He rubbed his temple. "Lisette is wrong-headed about the cause of our current situation. But, she's not wrong about the effect. I'm probably going to lose the house."

My father was under indictment in the RICO case Jason threatened. Whatever pull he had to stop it died with him. I still saw his wild eyes in my dreams. He would have killed me that night. Val had saved me in every way possible.

"I'm sorry," I said.

"Don't be," my father smiled. "I've still got a few more tricks up my sleeve. And I've set some things aside for you. Lisette doesn't know. You'll be okay, Willow."

"No," I said. "Don't set anything aside for me. Use it for your defense. Hell, use it to appease Lisette if that's what you want. I'll be all right."

Two days ago, I called my contact in New York. The internship he offered me was still available. I started at the end of the month.

"Are you sure?" he asked.

"I am." I reached for my father's hand. "It's the life I want. The life I was meant for. And I won't be alone."

A sad smile came over my father's face. He was still trying to grapple with everything that happened. News of Jason Soren's death had made all of my father's associates nervous. They were jumping ship, left and right. If convicted, my father might spend the next ten years or more behind bars. It tore at my heart, but he was ready for it. He was tired of running scared. Tired of having it hanging over his head. He wanted to pay the price for the choices he made, and I knew in my heart he would be okay.

"He's a good man?" Dad asked.

Val was the other thing he was still trying to process. I didn't know if my father knew the truth about Jason Soren and his nature. I hadn't yet found a way to tell him about Val's or mine. For now, it would stay our secret.

My love. My mate. My future.

He swore Jason hadn't paid him for me. It seemed that part of Jason's story was a lie. I wanted to believe my father. I wondered if perhaps Lisette was the real villain in this.

My father rose and put his arms around me. "I love you, Willow. Your mother named you right. You are strong. Adaptable. Just like she was. I'm going to make sure she's okay through this too."

I hugged him back. "You don't have to. I'm going to take care of her for you."

Somehow, I'd find a way to cover my mother's expenses at her nursing home in upstate New York. Next week, Val would come with me to visit her.

"Okay," he said. "We'll do it your way."

"Good. You just take care of you. You've got your hands full with your situation and with Lisette."

He raised a brow. "She is *not* adaptable, I'm afraid."

"No."

Calvin came to the doorway. "I'm sorry to interrupt. Miss Rousseau, your ride is here."

My ride. My heart flared with heat as I felt Val walk into the house. He appeared, strong, huge, handsome and steady. His eyes gave off that secret flash as he set them on me.

My father went to him and held out his hands. "Mr. Kalenkov," he said.

They'd met once before. After the chaos died down at the motel near Richmond, Val drove me to my father's house. News of Jason's death had already reached him. My father knew it was Val who saved my life.

"Mr. Rousseau," Val said. They shared a strong handshake.

"You ready?" Val smiled.

"I am," I said, rising. I went into Val's waiting arms. My father smiled. He had the hint of tears in his eyes, but he looked happy in spite of everything.

"We'll talk as soon as we can. It might not be for a while though. My lawyer thinks that's best," he said. "And don't believe everything you read on the internet about me in the meantime."

"I never have, Daddy," I said. I left Val's arms and hugged my father once again. He felt so good. So strong and big. I knew he wasn't scared, so neither was I.

Then, I took Val's hands and wiped away my own tears before they had a chance to fall.

I walked outside of my father's house for maybe the last time. I didn't know what the future held for him, but I knew my own was bright.

Val opened the passenger side door for me. I slipped inside the car and waved to my father.

"You sure you're ready to go?" Val asked.

I nodded, smiling. "Never been more sure of anything in my life."

I held Val's hand for the entire drive. I felt at peace with him. What I said was true. For the first time in my life, I felt like I was going toward something, instead of running away from it.

A little over an hour later, we arrived at the apartment I rented in Soho. I'd gotten the place for a relative steal. It was close to work, simple, mine.

Val walked me up. I had a decent view with a huge dormer window.

Val slid his hands around my waist and kissed my neck. Already, I burned for him. I felt that irresistible buzzing at the base of my neck.

Since Jason's death, we hadn't had much time alone together. Val worked with his crew to deal with all of Jason's pack members. Most were happy he was gone. But, it didn't mean Val or his family would trust them. He wouldn't tell me all of the details, but I knew many of them had been relocated to Canada. For those that could be rehabilitated, they were getting a fresh start.

"I love it here," I said. "I just wish you could move in with me right away."

"I do too," he said. "I've got a few things to settle with the firm. I've got a meeting with Payne in the morning."

"How do you think that will go?" I asked.

I knew Val felt unsettled. He hadn't trusted Payne with all his suspicions about Jason in the beginning, instead of relying on his own family. It could be a problem for Payne. Val might very well be out of a job this time tomorrow.

I turned to face him. His eyes reflected the full moon out the window. I ran my hands over his chest.

"It's going to be okay," I said. "I can feel it."

Val smiled. "I know. The thing is, ever since I met you, I've known that. Even after everything we've been through."

"I think I'm going to love it here," I said. "I mean I know it's not much more than a shoebox. But, it's mine. And you're mine too, Val."

There was something else between us. Val had been gentle

with me since that last night at the motel. So much had happened, I knew he was worried about either coming on too strong or scaring me. It suited me at first, but now as the dust settled and we were alone together, I knew I couldn't wait much longer.

"Val," I said. I slid my hands up his chest and touched his face. It seemed right that the moon was full. "Take me to the woods."

His eyes flashed. I felt his wolf stir. He didn't ask me if I was sure. Not then. I don't even remember walking out of the apartment or the drive to Central Park. I was too keyed up. So was he.

We found our way down a quiet trail in the North Woods as the night grew thicker. Part of me wished we'd flown to the place he was born, crazy as that sounded. Even here, I felt his pull to it.

He was Valentin Kalenkov. His Siberian blood flowed strong in his veins. He was impervious to the cold. The most powerful man I'd ever known. He was mine. Now, it was time at last, for me to become fully his.

Val came prepared. He brought a backpack and spread out a blanket. He found a secluded spot, so deep in the woods, it was hard to imagine we were so close to the city here.

If I was being honest, the danger of getting caught stirred my passion just that much more. We wouldn't though. Val knew what he was doing. He was born to protect me. It was in his blood as much as Russia was.

Someday, I knew he would take me there. I had a vision the other night. A dream. I saw a snowy landscape with a tucked away cabin on the hill. A sanctuary. A place we could escape to. And it was the place where my son would be born. That had been part of the vision too. He wasn't here yet, nor even close. But, he would be when the time was right.

"Come here," Val said, his voice low and sultry. Heat grew between my legs. I was already so wet for him. I had been since the moment he took my hand back at the apartment.

"Are you sure, my love?" he whispered.

"I am," I said.

He kissed me, slow and deep letting his tongue explore. His hands roamed over me, circling my hips, guiding me down. He laid me on the blanket. The stars glittered behind his head.

He was my world. The stars and the moon.

I wriggled out of my jeans. Val did the same. I cast my bra and panties aside. Val hovered over me, stroking himself. His eyes glinted like two blue diamonds. His wolf was so close to the surface.

I spread my legs for him. He ran a finger over my slick folds. I gasped. Just that one touch. It was as if he flipped a switch. My body responded to his. I gushed for him.

"That's it." He gave me that wicked smile, loving how easily he could turn me on.

Then, he entered me. I brought my legs up, wrapping them around his hips. I gasped again at the size of him. He stretched me wide. He was so good. So powerful. All mine.

He moved in me. I dug my fingers into his shoulder. It heightened his pleasure. He liked the wild parts of me and would work to bring them out. He nipped my ear.

He reached between us, finding the most sensitive bud between my legs. With his cock deep inside of me, he worked me there. It was too much. It was everything. I reared up, feeling the first powerful pull of an orgasm.

"Not yet," I gasped.

"Yes, my love," he growled. "Now. Let go for me. Let me feel you come around me."

I did. Of course I did. With one touch, one whisper, Val would always make me respond to him. I knew it would get even better, even more intense after tonight. He called it the Rise. If I'd craved him before, it would be nearly insatiable now. Oh, God. I wanted that.

"Scream, baby," he said. "It's only just the two of us."

I did. My orgasm thundered through me. He pressed himself even deeper into me as I rode it through.

So good. So much. Everything.

He kissed a trail between my breasts and down my stomach. He pressed my knees flat and tasted my juices. Then, he slid his hands beneath my hips and turned me.

I knew what he wanted. God. I'd waited for this my whole life.

Val worked me again. I didn't think I could come again so quickly after that last orgasm. But, I was about to find out what the Rise really meant.

He kept me like that, on all fours as he pinched me gently, kneading my sensitive flesh in all the right ways.

I came for him again. It was as if he were the maestro and my pleasure, his instrument. Oh, I played all night for him.

I rode him. I let him take me up against a tree. I went back on all fours. I tasted him. We tried everything and it still wasn't enough.

Then, Val turned me. He guided me into position. Instinct took over and I arched my back. Val entered me again, keeping a steadying hand on my hips. My knees trembled. I knew I'd be sore in muscles I didn't even know I had in the morning.

I dropped my chin, letting my hair fall to the side. That aching pleasure grew at the base of my neck.

I drew in a sharp breath as Val's teeth scraped my skin. He started to thrust his hips, driving himself deep.

At the point of his climax, he marked me. There was just a flash of pain, then it spread to the most intense pleasure I'd ever felt.

The world fell away. There was only him. There was only

us. My heart stopped. An instant later, it started. Only this time, I knew it would never be just my own again.

I felt him everywhere. In my head. In my core. In my heart and soul.

We were one. My fated mate. Neither of us would ever be alone again.

Later, Val held me in his arms as we watched the sun slowly rise over the trees.

It was beautiful. Brilliant. Perfect.

"I love you," he whispered. "You've given me the greatest gift."

I touched his cheek. "The gift is mine, my love."

And it was.

CHAPTER TWENTY-THREE

Val

Payne met me in the firm's new office space in the Flatiron Building. We stood at the window, looking down at Fifth Avenue.

"The New York office will be good for the firm," I said. "It was a coup to get this space."

Things had been up in the air between us since I got back from Virginia. Leo had brought the others without consulting with Payne first. From the moment he hired us to work for him, I knew that had been his one reservation. He had a policy against hiring pack members, preferring to employ lone Alphas. Payne knew full well that pack loyalty would always trump company loyalty.

The Kalenkovs were a little different. My nephews and I didn't function as a pack, but we were still family. I regretted any trouble I'd caused for Leo and the others. But, I would never regret acting to protect my mate, no matter the fallout.

I decided to launch into it head-on.

"Look," I said. "I know I left a mess in my wake back in Virginia. There were probably better ways to handle Jason Soren that wouldn't have caused so much turmoil."

Payne kept his focus on the street below. "It's generally bad for business to kill the client, yes."

I winced. I knew this was coming. My main objective today was to keep the heat on me and away from my family. I could start again. I loved working for Wolfguard more than anything I'd ever done. And, it brought me to Willow. I owed Payne so much.

"He would have killed Willow. *She* was the client the moment we were hired."

"And she's your mate," Payne said. It wasn't a question. I knew Leo had filled him in on the highlights of what went sideways in Virginia. Still, he wanted to hear it all from me.

"Yes," I said, turning to him. "Willow Rousseau is my fated mate."

"You've marked her," he said. Again, it didn't seem like a question.

"I have."

The corner of Payne's mouth twitched. "Then, I'd say it's about damn time. I'm happy for you."

I was gearing up to start my speech. Payne's smile took me off guard. He put a firm hand on my shoulder.

"I know what it's like, man, don't forget. When I met my wife, Lena, well...let's just say it wasn't the most convenient time for either of us to get too attached."

I knew a little about Payne's mate, Lena. She worked in the Louisville headquarters. Along with Payne and her shifter brother, Mac, Lena had been one of the heroes of the War for Kentucky. They had freed the shifters of the state from a ruthless *Tyrannous Alpha* a few years back.

"I'm glad you did what you did," Payne said. "And I'm sorry it was my orders that put you in the position to do it."

I was floored. I came here fully expecting a dressing down.

"Payne, I don't know what to say."

He let out a great sigh. "Val, you remind me of me. You don't let too many people close. I know your family went through some things back in Russia before you came over. And I know how important your family is to you. It's one of the reasons I hired you. And it's the main reason I think it's time for you to take on a partnership role."

Again, he had me speechless.

"Payne," I said. "I pretty much thought you were going to fire me."

"I thought about it," he said, not missing a beat. "I'm not happy you didn't trust me with your suspicions about Soren in the first place. But, I know why you didn't. If it had been Lena...hell...a few years back it *was* Lena. The men I served with in Mammoth Forest back in Kentucky...we aren't pack, but they're my brothers. In your shoes, I might have gone to them first too."

"Thank you," I said. "It means a lot to me that you still have faith in me."

"What I have," he said, reaching into his back pocket. "Is this."

He handed me a key. "Welcome to *your* new office space," he said.

My jaw dropped. "You've got to be kidding."

"Your mate's here, right?" he asked.

"Um...yes. Willow's taken a job not far from here."

"Good. So it's settled. You'll run the New York office for me. For *us*."

"Thank you," I said. It seemed inadequate, but it was all I had. I swallowed past a lump in my throat.

"Don't thank me yet," he said. His expression grew grave. I let out a breath. There was one last thing we needed to discuss.

I had given Payne the disk Soren implanted in me. He had friends in northern Michigan in Wild Lake who were trying to analyze it. They had access to one of the only doctors in the world who specialized in shifter medicine.

"You know," he said. "I thought we'd have more time. Before the next war. No, that's not even it. I'm beginning to think it was wrong to believe what happened in Kentucky was the end of a war. I think it might have only been the beginning."

My heart felt cold. Payne was saying the things I had feared.

"I think you're right. Soren told me he *bought* Willow. Her father swears it wasn't from him and he had no idea who Jason meant. I'm pretty sure Rousseau doesn't even know shifters exist. He certainly didn't know Jason was one. So, there's someone else. Someone bigger than Rousseau or his mafia associates. The Ring Willow heard Soren talking about," I said. "Were you able to find out what it is? Who Soren was answering to?"

"Not exactly. I don't know if this Ring is an actual ring, or a person, many people...we just don't know yet. But that implant, it was sophisticated. The shifter doctor we sent it to had never seen anything like it. Whoever Soren was working with or for...they might be more dangerous than anything we've seen. So, I need men I trust working with me. If Jason Soren is what I suspect, just one head of a giant Hydra...things might get worse before they get better. You ready for that?"

I answered almost without thinking. I felt the truth thundering through me. "Yes," I said. "I don't ever want another shifter to go through what I did. If it's a war we need to bring, I'll be ready. And it'll be my honor to serve alongside you."

Payne's jaw tightened. He stuck out his hand and shook mine in a solid grip. He wasn't my brother. He wasn't pack. He wasn't even family. But, my loyalty to Payne and to Wolfguard was a pact I would honor for the rest of my life.

"Good," he said. "Now call up that mate of yours. I want to meet Willow. Lena does too. I have a hunch the two of them will make fast friends. God help us both."

That got the first genuine smile out of me. I slapped Payne on the back, pocketed the key he gave me. Then, the two of us walked out of the office...*my* office, together.

CHAPTER TWENTY-FOUR

Val

I loved her in her ripped jeans and trademark knit beanie. I loved her in nothing as she writhed beneath me and gasped my name. Tonight though, Willow descended the apartment stairs wearing a stunning, royal blue designer dress that hugged her curves and plunged low in front. A predatory growl escaped my lips as she got close. I wanted to devour her, keep her all to myself. But, this was her night as much as it was mine.

I leaned against the limo door, trying to keep my wolf from coming out.

Willow's eyes shone as she spotted me. She held a little silver clutch purse in her hand. She grabbed the flowing end of her dress and did a little curtsey in front of me.

"I brought your glass coach, Cinderella," I said.

"My, what big eyes you have," she whispered.

I laughed. "I think you're mixing up your fairytales."

"Mmm," she said, sliding her hands up my lapels. She straightened my bowtie. I kissed her, careful not to mess up her makeup. There would be plenty of time for that later. God. I had a vision of bending her over the kitchen counter of her apartment and seeing just what she wore under that blue dress.

"It matches your eyes," she said, running her hand down the fabric.

"You're getting good at that," I whispered.

The driver waited behind the wheel, keeping his eyes straight ahead as I helped Willow into the back seat.

"Good at what, my love?" she asked, her voice low and sultry.

"Reading my thoughts," I said. It was new. In the two months since I first claimed Willow, I'd marked her at least a half a dozen times since. Each time, our bond grew even stronger. Now, in the quiet, she could hear my thoughts if I opened them to her. It was the same for me.

I called for the driver to pull away. When I turned back to Willow, she had a strange look in her eyes. She was homesick.

"Baby?"

She blinked rapidly. "No...it's just...I thought it would be a long time before I rode in one of these again. And I mean...I don't need it. It's just, life has a funny way of working itself out."

"Well," I said. "Can't have the new mate of the head of the New York office of Wolfguard Inc. riding the subway to this."

She leaned in and kissed me. "I'm so proud of you, Val. You're amazing."

"So are you," I said. "So much so...I think I want to make this a short night."

I kissed my way down her neck. I grew bold, sliding a thumb beneath her bodice. Her nipple peaked for me. I felt her heat beneath the fabric. She gasped.

"Val!"

God, I loved that. She would rise for me from just a whisper. I knew her body like I knew my own. Every inch. Every curve. Every goosebump as I ran my tongue across her lip.

I never knew how good it would be to have my mate beside me. My heart beat for her. Her joy. Her sorrow. Her pain. I would go to the ends of the earth and back giving her everything she needed. Right now, she needed me. Badly.

I lost track of time. The driver pulled up in front of the Flatiron Building. Too soon. I thought about having him drive around the block again.

Willow's cheeks flushed with desire. Oh, I would enjoy sating it. Over and over. I would take her to new heights tonight. Willow let out a little moan as she read my mind.

"Come on," I said. I didn't wait for the driver to get the door. The cool, night air would do my mate good. She took my hand and we stepped outside.

It was all I could do to keep my hands off of her as we rode the elevator.

"What?" she said, seeing the mischief in my eyes.

I tried to keep my mind blank. I had two surprises for her tonight. The first would greet her as soon as the elevator doors opened.

When they did, her hands flew to her mouth.

"Val! Are you serious? You did this?"

"I did," I said, beaming.

I'd redone the lobby of the Wolfguard-New York offices. Willow's photographs adorned the walls. She'd been working on a cityscape series. She captured the glittering nightlife in unique, gorgeous detail. Now, her talented eye would be on display to some of the most powerful people in the city. I hadn't yet told her, but the receptionist was already fielding inquiries. Willow's first gallery showing at the end of the year would be a sellout; I was sure of it. And I was so damn proud of her. This night, and every night I was with her, I felt like I could conquer the world.

She was charming, effortless as she helped me work the room. Tonight was the office grand opening and it mattered that I made a good impression. With Willow on my arm, I couldn't help it. We were perfectly matched.

Payne and Lena were here. Willow took to her right away. I was glad she had a friend and confidant who knew what the life of a wolf's mate really was.

My brother Andre moved heaven and earth to get here. He was proud of me. And it didn't hurt that some of our potential new clients got to meet the head of the most powerful Russian wolf pack.

Payne was thrilled. More than once he told me how sure he was I was the right choice to lead this project. I more than anyone knew how important it was. We needed powerful allies if we were going to uncover who Soren's pack was working with.

But all of that faded into the background as I watched Willow work the room.

"She's stunning," Andre stood beside me. "And it's about time you found her."

"I'm so glad you're here," I said. We would need Andre's help too in the coming years. His two children, my niece and nephew, stood together at the back of the room. Milo smiled as his sister Grace whispered something in his ear. Grace could bring us one of the most powerful allies of all. She was married to a dragon shifter. That was one secret I had yet to share with even Willow.

"Does she know?" Andre asked. For a moment, I thought he was talking about his dragon son-in-law, Gideon.

"What?"

Andre patted my breast pocket. Damn him for being so wily. He felt the outline of the ring box I brought with me. I kept it close to my heart at all times, waiting for the perfect moment.

"No," I said. "Not yet."

"Well, I suggest you stop waiting for the perfect moment. I'd say it's now."

He was right. Willow caught my eye from across the room. She threw her head back, mid-laugh. Her eyes sparkled. Her cheeks flushed with that lust-filled secret we shared. I slipped her panties off her in the limo.

She bit her lip and nearly undid me.

"We're all here," Andre said. "Your family. Your new partners. And she got some good news she's about to share."

Sure enough, Willow moved toward me. Her eyes glistened with happy tears. Her thoughts reached me, elated, unbidden.

They're letting my father go!

I heard her thoughts ring through my head. Andre patted me on the back, sipped his gin and tonic then disappeared into the crowd.

I slipped an arm around Willow. As my guests mingled, I found a quiet, empty office and took her inside.

"How do you know?" I asked.

"They dropped the charges," she said. "I just got a text. One of the witnesses against him went south. Val, did you do this? Your family? Was it Payne?"

I shook my head. "No. No one's said anything to me."

Darkness came into her eyes. I knew she worried about Soren's reach from beyond the grave as much as Payne and I did. But, tonight was a night for celebration. My brother was right. Now was the perfect time.

"Let's just be happy for him for now," I said.

I kissed her. As our lips parted, I knew Willow already suspected what I was about. I went down on my knee anyway.

She put her hands over her mouth. Her tears fell freely as I opened the red velvet box and revealed a four-carat sapphire encircled with diamonds.

"Will you marry me, my love?" I asked.

She was my mate. My life. We were already bonded forever and I knew her mind. Still, it felt good to hear the words.

"Oh, yes!" she squealed as I slipped the ring on her finger.

Willow wore my mark. Now, she wore my ring. I sealed it with a kiss and swept her off her feet.

"Here, here!"

The chorus behind me took me by surprise. I'd been so focused on Willow, I didn't know we were being watched.

She giggled as I turned. My brother, my niece and nephews, and most of the men of Wolfguard looked on. They raised their glasses in a toast.

Later that night, I took Willow back to the North Woods of Central Park. We had our own secret place there now. I would take her so many other places as we shared our life. For now, this felt most special.

I made love to her. I tasted her sweetest honey. I marked her as mine all over again.

"Go," she said after the fourth or fifth time we made love. She lay naked on the blanket I brought, leaves stuck in her hair.

"Do it for me," she said. "I want to watch you."

Smiling, I let out a howl. In one fluid movement, I shifted, letting my wolf out as Willow had commanded.

We had battles to fight, she and I. There might yet be a war to come. But that night and every night, we would face it together. And we would win. I knew it in my soul.

I ran to the top of the nearest hill. With the moon and the

waterfall at my back, I raised my head. I declared my love for my mate in a primal howl that echoed around the world.

———

UP NEXT FROM KIMBER WHITE

Things are heating up for the Wolf-guard Protectors. Up next, follow Leo as he chases down an ancient relic that may hold the key to uncovering who or what The Ring really is. Oh, and there might just be a curvy, sassy, museum curator who gets in his way and stirs his inner Alpha. Rahr! Don't miss Echo of Magic, the next sizzling book in the Wolfguard Protector Series.

CLICK TO LEARN MORE

Sign up for my newsletter if you want to be the first to know about my new releases. You get a free ebook when you join. http://www.kimberwhite.com/newsletter-signup/

BOOKS BY KIMBER WHITE

Wolfguard Protectors

Shift of Fate

Echo of Magic

Kiss of Midnight

Dragonkeepers Series Page

Kissed by Fire

Tempted by Fire

Marked by Fire

Claimed by Fire

Freed by Fire

Mammoth Forest Wolves Series Page

Liam

Mac

Gunnar

Payne

Jagger

Wild Ridge Bears Series Page

Lord of the Bears

Outlaw of the Bears

Rebel of the Bears

Curse of the Bears

Last of the Bears

Wild Lake Wolves Series Page

Rogue Alpha

Dark Wolf

Primal Heat

Savage Moon

Hunter's Heart

Wild Hearts

Stolen Mate

Claimed by the Pack Series Page

The Alpha's Mark

Sweet Submission

Rising Heat

Pack Wars

Choosing an Alpha

The Complete Series Box Set

ABOUT THE AUTHOR

Kimber White writes steamy paranormal romance with smoldering, alpha male shifters and kickass heroines (doormats need not apply). She lives on a lake in the Irish Hills of Michigan with one neurotic dog, her sweet, handsome son, her fire-breathing warrior-princess of a daughter, and the most supportive husband any writer could hope to have (seriously, he just took said son, daughter, and dog out for a boat ride so she could finish this book in peace!).

She loves connecting with readers. Sign up for her newsletter for the latest word on her new releases. You'll get a free ebook as a welcome gift.

http://www.kimberwhite.com/newsletter-signup